How to fight Aliens

{ A GUIDE TO USING a LASER LANCE by B. HOBBLE }

Nº ① "The Head Whacker"

SWING FAST!

{ Try to catch your Alien by surprise }

awesome **STUFF**

To Laura, Sarah, Alice and Emily

Random House Australia Pty Ltd
20 Alfred Street, Milsons Point NSW 2061
http://www.randomhouse.com.au

Sydney   New York   Toronto
London   Auckland   Johannesburg

First published by Random House Australia 2005

National Library of Australia
Cataloguing-in-Publication Entry:

    Tulloch, Richard.
        Awesome stuff.

        For children aged 8–12 years.
        ISBN 1 74166 038 6.

        I. Title.

    A823.3

Cover illustration by Shane Nagle
Cover design by Jobi Murphy
Internal design and typesetting by Jobi Murphy
Printed and bound by Griffin Press, Netley, South Australia

10 9 8 7 6 5 4 3 2 1

Richard Tulloch

awesome STUFF

Illustrations by Shane Nagle

RANDOM HOUSE AUSTRALIA

introduction n. in-tro-duk-shun. Who, what, where and why you should read this story. English teachers say introductions should be exciting and make you want to read more. Right, here goes …

THIS is totally awesome! I used to think I was just a normal, average kid. Then suddenly I'm Brian Hobble, soccer hero, Z Squad fighter and TV star. I've been freaked out by a haunted pink pen, chased by zombie bikies and I've dropped into a crowded shopping mall wearing fairy wings.*

But the most amazing thing so far has been discovering the fantastic power of my writing. It turns out I'm a genius! I'm Brian (Super Brain) Hobble, the most amazing creative writer ever to come out of Garunga District School. I can make people laugh or cry. If I put the right words in an email, I can make girls … um (deep breath in – excuse me while

---

* Note: In case you don't know what I'm talking about, those things happened in my other stories, *Weird Stuff* and *Freaky Stuff*, which my friends reckon are the best things ever written in our Solar System. Lancelot Cummins liked them too. I met him when he came to our school. Lancelot Cummins is a professional author who wrote fantastic books like *Nose Job*, *Zombie Squad* and *Escape from Planet Zog*, so if Lance says my stories are good he must be right.

1

I suck on my asthma puffer here) ... I can make girls fall in love. With me!

I'm also completely, utterly, amazingly brilliant at making up lies. My lies are so unbelievable that everyone believes them. I can think of totally watertight excuses and cast-iron alibis, which save me and my friends the bother of doing our homework. I can concoct visionary, inspired, ingenious, innovative, inventive, original stories. (You may notice I use impressive words like 'concoct' and 'visionary'. I found them in my big thick thesaurus, and if you put words like that into stuff you write, everyone thinks you must be awesomely clever.)

But we powerful writers have a choice to make. We can use our talents to make the world a better place, or we can use them for selfish, wicked purposes. If I want to, I could become an evil genius like Dr Overcoat in Lancelot Cummins' *Zombie Squad* books. Or I could think up dastardly plans like Professor Mucus in *Nose Job*, and cover the whole world in snotty green slime.

I have to admit, once or twice I used my writing genius for evil purposes. I lost control and got carried away for a while. I'm totally, completely, utterly ashamed of the wicked things I did in this new adventure, though it was kind of fun being bad. Until I made a total, complete, utter idiot of myself. Now, because I've become a brave and honest writer (as well as being brilliant), I have to tell you about it.

In this new, weird, totally freaky, absolutely true story, I use my brilliant brain to save myself when I'm hanging off a massive wall by my fingertips. I use a laser lance to fight my best friend who's turned into a vicious alien. And most amazingly of all, I write love poems ... and they work!

In fact, as you read this story, you'll notice something totally *awesome*. Every one of my fabulous schemes works unbelievably well ... for a while.

Then things start to go horribly wrong.

Read on, Brian Hobble fans ...

IF YOU DARE!

mythomania *n. mith-o-may-nee-ya.* When you tell lies, myths, fibs, stories and untruths which are so bizarre that only a maniac would believe them.

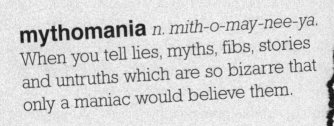

> Dear Mr Mackington,
> Vince writ a real good poem for homework, but his guinee pig ate it. Pleese let him off.
> Signed, Mrs Peretti (His Mum)

'No way will Mr Mackington believe that excuse, Vince!' I said.

'I used "My dog ate my homework" last time, Brian. I can't use it again.'

Mr Mackington set us this English assignment: 'Make up a short poem on the theme of Beauty'. It was hard, and I was worried about what kids would think when they heard my beauty poem. Vince hadn't been able to think of anything that was beautiful. Besides, he'd been too busy, watching a soccer match on TV. 'This will be three projects in a row I haven't done, Brian. I'll get detention for sure.'

'Well, the guinea pig's hopeless,' I said. 'You might as well say your pet gorilla ate your homework.'

'I haven't got a pet gorilla; only Chompy the guinea pig.' Vince shrugged, palms facing up, like he was holding a pizza in each hand. Sometimes you could really tell he was from an Italian family.

'Make up something else, Vince.'

'I'm no good at making stuff up. Please, Brian, please help me!' Vince fell to his knees in front of me and clasped his hands like a beggar. (I'm exaggerating here, which is something we writers are allowed to do. Vince didn't exactly fall to his knees, but he punched my arm in a begging sort of way.) 'Brian, you're my best mate. I'm not asking you to write my poem for me, just a real good excuse. Everyone reckons you're a creative genius. And your writing's sort of scribbly like my mum's.'

Sometimes it was hard being a writer. I'd had a few stories published in the *Garunga School Gazette*, so now everyone assumed I'd make up something great every time I picked up a pen. Writing an excuse note was a new challenge. I had no idea if I could write one good enough to fool a smart teacher like Mr Mackington.

Vince pleaded, 'You write my note and I'll lend you my DeathTrap game for the weekend.'

'Two weekends,' I said. I could get into serious trouble for forgery. I needed something good in return.

5

'You got me, Brian. I'll agree to anything!'

'*Anything*, Vince?' A clever thought had just popped into my head.

There's a great book by my favourite author, Lancelot Cummins, called *Think Twice*. It's about a boy called Graham who grows a second brain, more brilliant than his normal one. Graham's new brain makes great suggestions which help him solve his problems. When Vince said he'd agree to anything, it was like I had an amazing second brain which suddenly tapped me on the shoulder with a smart idea. 'You have Vincent Peretti in your power, Brian,' my new brain whispered. 'Now you can make him do whatever you want. And the thing you want him to do is ...'

'Hey, that's perfect!' I whispered back.

'What's perfect, Brian?' asked Vince.

'Forget about lending me DeathTrap, Vince. I'll write you an excuse note if you promise to come to DAGS with me.'

'DAGS?'

'You know, D-A-G-S. It stands for "Drama At Garunga School".'

'You're doing drama, Brian?'

'There's a new workshop starting after school tomorrow. I told them I'd go.'

'Who's "them"?'

'Just some people, Vince.'

'All the nerdy useless social reject kids are in DAGS, Brian. What people?'

'People' was Cassie Wyman, the cutest girl in the entire history of the Universe, but I didn't want even my best friend to know I liked her. Cassie Wyman had invited me to join DAGS, and I'd agreed.

Drama scared me stupid, especially DAGS, where I'd probably be the only boy in the group. But I said yes because it was Cassie Wyman who asked me. I'd have said yes if Cassie invited me to spend ten years with her in the Great Bog of Zog (the most disgusting place in the Galaxy, according to a Lancelot Cummins book).

Cassie was my girl friend. My girl friend, but not my *girlfriend*. That little gap between 'girl' and 'friend' made all the difference. My girl friend liked me, and often came around to my place to work on school projects. There was lots of talk, but that was all. I'd never been brave enough to ask if she thought I was a hot, spunky, attractive, appealing super-hunk. The cute kind of guy you'd want as your *boyfriend*.

Cassie was nice to me, the way she was nice to everyone, even 'social rejects' like Madeline Chubb. 'Social rejects make the best friends,' Cassie laughed when I asked her about this. 'They're always there when you want them, and they appreciate anything you do for them.' I laughed with her, but uncomfortably. I was afraid she might have *me* in her social reject friend category too.

The past fortnight we'd had no new projects to work on. The only way to see Cassie outside school would have been to ask her to a movie, on a real *date*. I didn't have the nerve for that. It would have killed me if she said 'no'.

So when Cassie asked me to go to DAGS, I said 'yes' in two-squillionths of a second, and straight after that, I promised her I'd bring some other boys along. I tried to give her the impression that all the guys at Garunga would rush to join DAGS if they knew Brian Hobble was going. So far I hadn't been able to talk anybody into it, but now I had Vince in my power.

'No way am I doing drama!' said Vince.

'Do you want me to write your excuse note or not?'

'Okay,' said Vince. 'I'll come to DAGS. But if it's no good I'm walking out, man.'

'It'll be really good,' I promised. 'They're getting a new director, Cassie said ... I mean, people told me.' I pulled a writing pad from my bag. 'Okay, your excuse note ...'

'This sure better be good, Brian,' muttered Vince. 'I can't believe we're going to DAGS!'

He peered over my shoulder as I waved my hand creatively above the blank white paper. At times like that it would be good to have a special wicked pen which could think up evil lies for you.

'How about we make your grandma get sick?' I said.

'No good,' said Vince.

'Or dead. Maybe you had to go to her funeral.'

'I've already been to three grandmas' funerals this year. If a fourth one dies, it'll look suspicious.'

I swear, this new business of thinking up excuses was harder than doing homework. Especially thinking up excuses for Vince, who'd already used all the normal ones. Then suddenly my brilliant new brain came back from a short coffee break.

'I've got it, Vince!' I said, 'The Ethnic Excuse!'

Vince scratched the top of his head. That mop of fuzzy dark hair clearly got in the way of him being clever like me. 'What's the Ethnic Excuse, Brian?'

'You remember how Grace Tan and Simon Cheung got a day off school for Chinese New Year?'

'So?'

'So your family's Italian. When do Italians have a national holiday?'

Vince thought for a moment, then clicked his fingers. 'When we win the soccer World Cup!'

'You wish!' I said. I scribbled a few lines in my notepad:

Dear Mister Mackington,

Please you excuse our boy Vincent for not doing his poem. Yesterday was Romeo Ravoli Day, when we have holiday to remember Italy (our country) war against Hungary.

Vincent promise on his grandmothers' graves to write his poem next week (or maybe the week after).

Signed, Mrs Signor Peretti

Vince punched his fist into my arm like I'd just kicked a winning goal. 'Brian, mate, you're a genius!'

'I know,' I said.

'It's exactly like what Mama would write. It will fool him for sure.' Vince punched me again. 'For sure!' He punched me once more.

'Thanks, Vince,' I said, modestly rubbing my arm

and scratching a little itch on my nose. I had just been awesomely clever. Mr Mackington wouldn't be able to ask Vince tricky questions about the Ethnic Excuse, in case that seemed like racial discrimination against Italians.

Vince stuffed the note into his backpack. 'Brian, do we *have* to go to DAGS? I really don't reckon I'll be any good at this drama stuff. I don't want to be the worst in the class ...'

I had to stop Vince wriggling out of our agreement, and suddenly my brain made another smart suggestion. 'Why don't you tell Seven Eleven he has to come too?'

Seven Eleven was Sean Peters. He was a bit of an idiot, but Vince and I kind of liked him. We called him 'Seven Eleven' because he never stopped talking. His mouth was like an all-night store, open any time.

'Great idea, Brian!' grinned Vince. 'Seven Eleven's never done drama either. We'll look better if he comes too.'

I twisted away before he could land another punch on my sore arm, and sauntered off, hands in my pockets, whistling casually like nothing special had happened.

Inside my head, my brilliant second brain did a handspring, ripped off its shirt and bowed to an imaginary cheering crowd. What a morning I'd had! I'd helped my best friend, and now I'd be able to impress Cassie Wyman too. The more boys I could get along to DAGS, the more I'd show Cassie Wyman what a popular, leader-of-the-pack sort of guy I was. Not a desperate social reject who didn't dare ask a girl out on a date.

Ah, it made you feel so good to be clever! Maybe the evil Zoggian General Klag felt like this after dreaming up his scheme to block the world's toilets so they'd overflow and pollute the cities (in Lancelot Cummins' book *Escape from Planet Zog*).

I scratched my itchy nose again and wondered if Mr Mackington really would accept the Ethnic Excuse. He'd have to, wouldn't he? And with a bit of luck, DAGS wouldn't be too bad. I couldn't afford to have my friends hate me for getting them into something totally embarrassing.

drama n. drar-muh. Acting, theatre, putting on plays. (Note: drama can also mean where stuff goes wrong, and everyone gets over-emotional and totally loses it. **Drama queens** are show-offs.)

THERE was a red spot on the end of my nose next morning. I hoped it wouldn't grow into a zit. I wanted to look my best for DAGS.

It was the first time I'd done drama. I'd acted in two plays, but that was years ago. Anyway, you couldn't describe Kindergarten Green's production of *Little Red Riding Hood* as 'doing drama'. I'd only played the part of a rock, kneeling on the stage so Little Red could plonk her backside on me when she needed a rest. DAGS acting was sure to be harder than rock acting.

'You'll fit in just fine, Brian,' said Cassie Wyman, flashing me an encouraging smile as we walked down to the gym. Oh dear, I wished I dared to tell her how gorgeous she was!

'Oh, I know I'll be a great actor,' I said jokingly, 'me being so, um, good-looking ...'

BRIAN HOBBLE'S GUIDE to ACTING expressions

1. Cool

2. Angry

3. Sad { like my friend has been killed by Aliens }

4. Relieved { ...that it wasn't me who got killed }

5. Oops! (I forgot my next line)

I held my breath and avoided her eye. I'd just given Cassie a clever cue. Now if she wanted to, she could make the scene go like this:

Cassie: You really *are* so good-looking, Brian. You're a fantastically handsome super-hunk! I think you are so hot! I

> want you to take me in your manly arms
> right now ...'

Me: Well, okay Cassie ... but we're at
school. People are watching.

Cassie: I don't care, Brian. (*She yells loudly*)
You are so cute, I want the whole world to
know that you're my super-sexy ***boyfriend***!

Unfortunately she didn't say that. Cassie flicked
back her blonde ponytail and looked thoughtfully
into my face. I quickly covered my nose zit with
what I hoped was a casual finger. She said,
'Seriously, Brian, you don't have to be good-looking
to do drama.' Ouch! Did this mean she didn't think
I was attractive enough to be her boyfriend?

What she said next made me feel even worse.
'You were great as that Sucking Squeezee Kid.'

A short stabbing pain went through me. It did
whenever I was reminded of my embarrassing
appearance in that TV ad. (I wrote about it in
Freaky Stuff, but after that I tried to delete it from
my brain's hard drive.)

'You looked so pathetic and skinny and uncool,'
Cassie giggled. 'You were perfect in the part.'

'Yeah,' I said miserably. Pathetic, skinny, uncool
Brian Hobble. Cassie Wyman was only being my
friend because she felt sorry for social rejects. And
maybe because I was useful to her.

'Did you get some other boys to come to DAGS?'
she asked.

'Vince Peretti and Sean Peters,' I muttered. Yes, you could count on good old Brian (Mr Reliable) Hobble to keep his promises.

'Oh well done you! That's four boys at least. I invited Nathan Lumsdyke too.'

This was getting worse and worse. Not only was Nathan Lumsdyke a real nerd, but he was a real nerd who was trying to worm his way into Cassie's life. There he was, waiting for her outside the gym.

'Hello there, Cassie,' he chirped. 'The Drama room's actually still locked. Cassie, I actually think DAGS will be rather good this term, actually. I looked up the guest director on the internet actually. Her name is Elly Gerballo and she played Lady Macbeth in *Shakespeare by the Lake*. Actually, Cassie, you'd be very interested in this ...'

He adjusted his glasses and elbowed his way in between me and Cassie. Then he took over talking to her as she joined Madeline Chubb and some other girls filing into the gym.

As I shuffled after them, a mocking voice behind me called, 'Hey guys, look who's going to DAGS!' Kelvin Moray, my worst enemy, who thought he was the coolest, toughest kid in the school, was perched on the hill overlooking the path with his hangers-on Rocco Ferris and big Arthur Neerlander.

I pretended not to notice them. 'Think you're a bit of an actor, do you Brian?' called Rocco.

'Nah,' sneered Kelvin, 'going to DAGS is the

only way a social reject like Brian might get a girl-friend.' Ouch! Kelvin was an idiot, but this time I was glad Cassie didn't hear him.

I slipped into the gym, and was relieved to find Vince there already. He was lurking in the background, testing his muscles on the low holds of the new rock-climbing wall, trying not to listen to what Sean (Seven Eleven) Peters was gushing into his ear. 'Drama isn't just about acting different characters,' said Sean. 'My big sister says it's about tapping your creativity in a safe and supportive environment, and revealing your Inner Child ...'

Sean had recently started an amazing growth spurt. He used to be just a bit taller than Vince and me, but suddenly he was this great gangling giraffe who towered over us. There was room inside the new Sean Peters for two Inner Children, standing one on top of the other. Sean continued: 'My sister says as we get older we try to hide our Inner Child under a veneer of sophistication ...'

'Your sister sure talks a load of bull, Seven Eleven,' said Vince.

It sounded like bull to me too, although Sean Peters was sometimes right. I hoped that at DAGS I wouldn't be asked to reveal my Inner Child, and remind people what I'd been like as a little kid. My Inner Child used to wet his bed, suck his thumb, and once kissed Madeline Chubb in the Little School sandpit.

17

There were fifteen DAGS milling around the gym. Eleven girls and four boys. From our year there was Madeline, Sean, Vince and I, and still talking to Cassie of course was Nathan Lumsdyke. There were a number of other girls I didn't know.

The new drama director arrived. 'Sorry to keep you waiting, guys,' she called and bustled across to unlock the Drama room door. Her shock of red hair was tied back in a floral scarf. She wore loose green track pants and a black t-shirt with a slogan across her chest: *Press my PLAY button.*

We filed into the Drama room. A line of mirrors covered a whole wall. I could see my nose reflected in them. It was a bit red from all my scratching. Luckily nobody else in DAGS was looking at my nose. They were watching the drama director as she plastered a sticker onto the middle of her forehead: *ELLY.* She looked like a total idiot.

'Hi guys, I'm Elly Gerballo.' She smiled and held up her hand in mock salute.

'Hi, Elly Gerballo,' said Madeline Chubb. She held up her hand in an answering salute. Nobody else spoke, although Vince glanced at me, stuck his finger down his throat and mimed throwing up.

'We're going to play some games to start with,' said Elly. 'They might seem like kiddy games to you big sophisticated dudes, but they'll help us get to know each other, have some fun, and reveal our

Inner Child.' Sean Peters tapped the side of his nose and winked at me.

Elly passed out felt pens. Two minutes later we all looked like total idiots, with our first names scrawled on stickers on our foreheads: *BRIAN, VINCE, NATHAN, CASSIE, SEAN, LEEANNE, SIOUX, JULIE* ... and *MADELI*. Madeline Chubb couldn't fit her whole name on her sticker.

Next we had to take off our shoes and walk around the room, introducing ourselves to everyone we bumped into, shaking hands, looking them in the eye and reading their name stickers. It seemed corny to be introducing myself to people I'd known for years: 'Hello Vince, I'm Brian ... Hello Madeli, I'm Brian ... Hi Cassie ...' I also came face to face with some of the girls I didn't know. 'Hello Leeanne ... Hello Sox ... oh, you pronounce that *Sue*, do you? Sorry, Sioux.'

I found that after a couple of minutes I could remember everybody's name. Everyone seemed to remember mine too.

Then we sat on gym mats in a circle and tried to tell a group story, with each person only saying one word at a time, then letting the next person add a word: 'A ... man ... was ... walking ... down ... the ... street ... when ... he ... saw ... a ... big ... fat ... large ... toilet ... so ... he ... said ... stop ... jumping ... up ...'

It took a few tries before we got the stories to flow,

19

but soon the words started flipping round the circle faster and faster and we cackled with laughter as we thought up ridiculous adventures.

'A-boy-called-Jack-was-very-scared-of-Tyrannosaurus Rexes ...'

'Cauliflower-grows-in-big-bunches-in-Mrs Davenport's-underpants ...'

I'd thought that DAGS might be revoltingly embarrassing and hoped my friends wouldn't think *I* was embarrassing for getting them involved. But Sean Peters rocked around on the gym mat hooting. Vince grinned and punched me on the arm again. DAGS was turning out to be fun!

mime *n. mym.* Making something that isn't really there look like it is there.

THEN Elly showed us how to do mime. 'I'm going to take an imaginary object,' she said, 'and without talking, I'll try to show you what it is.' She reached beside her and picked up a mimed ball. 'It can be heavy or light, hard or soft, hot or cold. It can be big, or tiny . . .'

As she talked, her hands moved around the ball. There was no ball, except as we watched Elly's hands, we could see it. We watched it grow from golf ball size, to become a heavy cannon ball she could hardly lift, then as she put it to her lips and blew air into it, the cannon ball changed into a balloon she could balance on a finger. It was incredible, magic stuff! I could see the balloon. I totally believed in the balloon – but there was nothing there.

Elly flicked the balloon with her finger and it floated across to Cassie Wyman, sitting next to her. Cassie waited till the balloon settled in her hands,

21

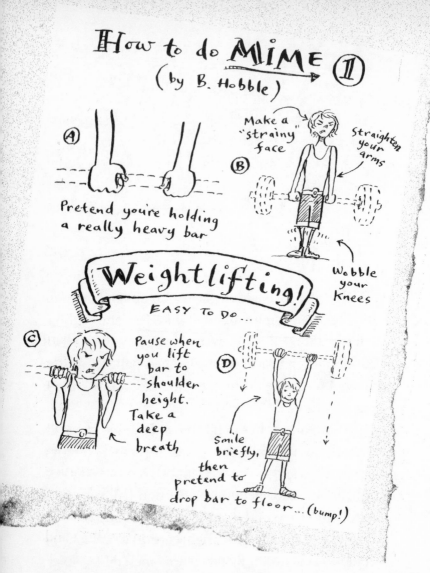

How to do MIME ①
(by B. Hobble)

Ⓐ Pretend you're holding a really heavy bar

Ⓑ Make a "strainy" face

Straighten your arms

Wobble your knees

Weightlifting!

EASY TO DO...

Ⓒ Pause when you lift bar to shoulder height. Take a deep breath

Ⓓ Smile briefly, then pretend to drop bar to floor... (bump!)

then began to stroke it. And it changed again. More magic!

'What's Cassie made it into?' asked Elly quietly.

'A cat!' whispered a few people.

Cassie carefully passed the invisible cat to Nathan

Lumsdyke. In Nathan's hands the cat shrank to something tiny, held between his finger and thumb. He made a series of tight little tugging actions. 'It's a needle!' Cassie called out, delighted. Oh no, even nerdy Nathan Lumsdyke was good at drama!

Help me now, new clever brain, I urged. *I don't want to look like a complete total idiot when I have to do my action. You've got less than two minutes to think up something brilliant!*

The mimed object moved around the circle, becoming a spade (Julie), then a pipe (Kaytlyn), a sub-machine gun (Sean Peters), a towel (Sioux), another sub-machine gun (Vince Peretti) ...

Each move brought it closer to me. My heart thumped. My breath came in shallow gasps. I desperately wanted to think of something hilarious, or sensitive, or intelligent, or at least original. Something to show Cassie and these other DAGS what a brilliant, daring, creative brain I had. But as my turn approached, my brilliant, daring, creative brain was running round in panic-stricken circles, picking up ideas and throwing them away again.

Madeline Chubb had the mimed object now and was turning it into something round. 'A football!' guessed Vince. Madeline shook her head. 'A basketball?' asked Julie. 'No,' said Madeline. 'A severed head with blood dripping off it?' 'You're being silly, Sean Peters,' said Madeline.

I took a quick puff on my asthma inhaler, but

there seemed to be a small Zoggian alien stuck in my throat, crushing my windpipe with his wiry green fingers. I was next and my brain was on strike.

'Maybe you should tell us what it is, Madeli,' said Elly.

'It's a lettuce,' said Madeline Chubb and passed it to me.

I held the lettuce in my hands and stared at it. My mind was a complete blank. I opened my hands and moved them slightly apart. The invisible lettuce became longer ... and thinner. Wonder of wonders, an idea popped into my head! A brilliantly fantastic idea. 'Brian Hobble, I can make you a drama genius!' whispered my brand new clever brain. I wrapped the invisible thing around my neck.

'I actually think it's a scarf, actually,' said Nathan Lumsdyke.

'It's not a scarf,' I said. He'd actually been right, but I didn't want Nathan to be the one to get the answer. Besides, as he spoke my brain thought of something even more clever and original. I turned the scarf into a boa constrictor. A huge, powerful boa constrictor, which was strangling me. My hands clutched at it, trying to prise it from my throat. I gasped for breath, eyes rolling, tongue hanging out. I fell back on the gym mat and writhed in agony, fighting the massive snake as my life ebbed away. My body arched. My heels thumped and my legs thrashed, but I wasn't strong enough. The boa constrictor won. My body collapsed, limp and lifeless.

I lay still for a moment, letting the brilliance of my acting performance settle around the Drama room. Then I sat up again. Everybody was staring at me.

'Anybody like to guess what Brian was doing?' said Elly.

Nobody spoke. They were obviously stunned into silence by my magnificent acting. Then a few people made nervous guesses.

'Were you having some sort of fit, Brian?' asked Cassie Wyman.

'An asthma attack!' said Madeline Chubb.

I shook my head. This wasn't meant to happen! Maybe my brilliant mime performance wasn't as clear to everyone else as it was to me. Had I done something wrong?

'Tell us please, Brian,' said Elly gently.

'I was being strangled by a boa constrictor,' I said.

'Oh, I *see*!' smiled Elly. 'Very energetic, Brian. Very brave performance. Would you like to pass the boa constrictor to Leeanne and let her have a turn now?'

Cassie flashed me a dazzling, encouraging smile; the sort that made me feel like my guts had been sucked out by a small alien. Nathan smiled too, only his smile was more of a nasty, superior, evil-warlord-style smirk.

As we came close to the end of the workshop, Elly

How to do MIME ②
(by B. Hobble)

Being stuck in a Cage!!

HARDER TO DO...

Try to make yourself sweat

Stare wildly into space

grit teeth

THINK SAD Stuff

Imagine RATS nearby

Imagine you are starving to death

Gerballo peeled the sticker off her forehead. I'd become so used to it I'd forgotten how strange it had looked at first. 'In here on the mats for a moment, guys,' she said. She thanked us all for coming and hoped we'd enjoyed ourselves. 'It's been my first time teaching kids for a while, so I guess I was nervous too, but you guys have been great to work with. Thanks.'

She clapped us, and we clapped her too. We all really liked Elly now.

'At the end of term we're putting on a play, so

next week we'll start preparing for that,' said Elly. 'We're very lucky. A rather special author is going to write the play for us to perform.' She moved across to the door, opened it, beckoned, and in he walked. 'Who's read books by Lancelot Cummins?' asked Elly.

Nobody could believe it! Lancelot Cummins, the greatest writer in the Universe, author of top books like *Nose Job*, *A T-Rex Ate My Homework* and *Think Twice*, was writing a play for us to do at DAGS! He looked more relaxed than when he'd been our school's writer-in-residence earlier in the year. His grey hair and beard were still neatly trimmed, but he wore jeans and sneakers, and peeping out from under his jacket was a black *Zombie Squad* t-shirt.

He nodded to Nathan Lumsdyke, then caught my eye. His face crinkled into a broad grin and he gave me a big thumbs up. 'Hello again, Brian.' I was glad people saw me being recognised by a famous children's author. When I say 'people' I mean Cassie of course. I smiled at her and she smiled back. Then I smirked at Nathan.

Elly clapped her hands to get attention. 'We're very lucky to have Mr Cummins working with us,' she announced. 'I'm sure you all love his books and it's great that he's chosen DAGS to do the first production of his brand new play. Maybe you'd like to tell us about it, Mr Cummins?'

'Um,' he said, 'the first thing I need to tell you is

to call me Lance, not Mr Cummins. This is not school. I'm the writer and you're the actors and we're all going on a journey of discovery together. The second thing I have to say is that my play's not finished yet. I'll be adding a few scenes each week until we have a whole show. It's very important for a playwright to see and hear the lines read by actors. My work is never as good as I want it to be the first time I write it, so expect lots of things to change as the rehearsals go on.

'My play is called *Cyberno*, and I've based it loosely on a classic old play, although I'm afraid I'm giving it the Lancelot Cummins treatment, and setting it in space. On Planet Zog.'

'Oh yuck!' said Vince. 'We'll have to bring clothes pegs to rehearsals!'

People laughed. In the book *Escape from Planet Zog*, Captain Loopy's crew wear clothes pegs on their noses because of the stench. We all knew Planet Zog was the most revolting place in the Universe, full of farting gas geysers, stinking slime swamps and oceans of pus.

'There'll be interesting parts for everyone,' said Elly, 'but so that Lance and I can see what kind of characters you each like playing, we'd like everyone to prepare a short audition piece and show it to us next week.' She handed out little books. 'Choose your audition piece from this book, *Try Out*. Look for something that suits the sort of person you are, or if you'd prefer to do a speech from another play, we'd love to see that. Learn your piece if you have time, but otherwise it's fine just to read. Thanks for coming everybody, and I hope it was fun!'

It had been fun. Sort of scary, but fun. As we left the room, I caught sight of myself in the mirror. I realised that while we'd been doing drama a whole hour had passed, and I hadn't thought once about how I was pathetic, skinny and uncool. With a zit on the end of my nose.

Now I had until next week to rehearse a great audition piece, and get a cool part in the play. At the very least, I was determined to do better than Nathan Lumsdyke.

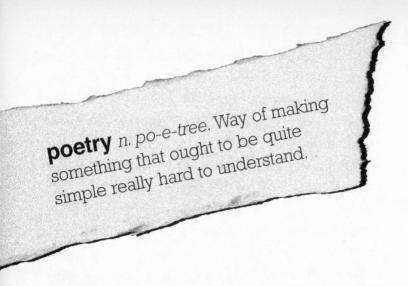

poetry n. po-e-tree. Way of making something that ought to be quite simple really hard to understand.

'POETRY!' announced Mr Mackington. 'The spontaneous overflow of powerful emotions! Poems can amuse us, shock us, surprise us, or make us fall in love. Let's hear yours, Brian Hobble.'

I knew he'd choose me to read my poem to the English class. Now that I was supposed to be good at writing, I often got picked first, to set an example to my creatively challenged classmates.

I'd almost got used to reading my work, but this time I'd written something awkward. My powerful emotions spontaneously overflowed as I stood up at my table, and I knocked my chair over backwards. Suddenly the classroom seemed to grow hotter. It was like the time in *Escape from Planet Zog* when the inquisitors put Captain Loopy in the Fart Oven and turn the methane meter up to 200,000,000 degrees. Sweat squirted off my forehead and dripped onto the paper. My heart was trying to escape out through my ribs. *Thump-thump, thump-thump!*

You see, my beauty poem was about Cassie Wyman. You know by now that I like Cassie a lot. I avoided looking anywhere near her as I read it out loud.

'Your beautiful eyes, as you move with such grace
Your beautiful hair frames your beautiful face,
The beautifullest thing that I've seen for a while
Is your beautiful smile.'

'Derrrrrr!' went Kelvin Moray, and 'Derrrrrr!' went his stupid friends Arthur Neerlander and Rocco Ferris.

'Nice work, Brian,' said Mr Mackington. 'I like the way you've repeated the "beautiful"s.' Then like a true Zoggian inquisitor he turned up the heat. 'Who is your poem about?'

'Um ...' I said.

I was totally trapped, like when the inquisitors direct the sun's rays onto Captain Loopy's navel through a giant magnifying glass. I didn't dare think how Cassie would react if I said I'd written my poem about her. And my friends and enemies would totally pay me out for the rest of my miserable life. Then I suddenly had another fantastic Brian Hobble Creative Brainwave. I said, 'My poem's about my grandma.'

Thank you, oh my brilliant brain! I thought. That was such a fantastic lie! It would show everyone, including Cassie, that I was a sensitive, intelligent guy who could see beauty in old people. She was smiling at me now, as I modestly scratched the itch on my nose.

The Fart Oven was turned off and I sat down, cool as a frozen Icy Pop stick. It would have looked even cooler if I'd remembered to pick up my chair before I sat on it.

Kelvin Moray opened his mouth to 'derr' me, but Mr Mackington jumped in first. He was one of those smart teachers who can see into the future and stop trouble before it starts. 'Maybe you'd be so kind as to share *your* poem with us, Mr Moray?' he said firmly.

Kelvin smirked, glanced sideways at Rocco and Arthur, slid to his feet and read:

'*Beauty*, by Kelvin Moray

There was a young beauty called Jude

Who ran down the street in the nude.

A cheeky young feller,

Took out his umbrella

And –'

Mr Mackington glided across the classroom like he was wearing jet-propelled space skates, and snatched Kelvin's paper before he could read any more.

'Whooo!' from Arthur and Rocco, and giggles from Abby and Sarah and Sofie. Those three girls thought anything Kelvin Moray did was hilarious. They had brains made of bubblegum.

'That will do,' snapped Mr Mackington. 'You

didn't write that yourself, did you Kelvin?' Kelvin shrugged but said nothing. 'You can stay behind after school and write me an original poem.'

I winked at Vince Peretti across the table. Vince tried to stifle a laugh by sticking the back of his hand in his mouth. A sound like a Zoggian spaceship taking off seemed to squeeze out through his ears. Bad move, Vince, I thought. Never draw attention to yourself when you haven't done your homework.

'And where's your poem, Mr Peretti?' Mr Mackington was doing his inquisitor act again.

Vince stopped laughing. He reached into the depths of his backpack and handed Mr Mackington my crumpled Ethnic Excuse note. Mr Mackington smoothed it out and stared at it for some time, lips pushed forward and pressed together. Then he folded it neatly and tucked it into his folder. 'I'm sure we'd all like to hear a bit more about this special Italian holiday of yours, Vince. What is it called again?'

Uh-oh! The inquisitor was testing Vince on the finer details of Romeo Ravoli Day. Vince looked helplessly across the table at me. I pretended to be busy editing my poem, angling my body so that Mr Mackington couldn't see what I was writing.

'This Italian holiday is called ... ?' repeated Mr Mackington.

I held up my writing pad so Vince could read what I'd written: *ROMEO*.

'Alfa Romeo Day, Sir,' said Vince.

'Ah, that was it,' said Mr Mackington. Lucky for Vince he didn't cross-check with the excuse note. 'You had no time for writing poetry on Alfa Romeo Day because you were so busy.'

'For sure, Sir,' nodded Vince.

'Busy doing what, Vince?'

'Well, Sir ... my family had this big party, Sir, an ethnic one. With all this Italian food and drink and dancing and singing and ... um, praying ...'

'It sounds like terrific fun, Vince,' smiled Mr Mackington. 'And you Italians do this to remember ... what was it again ... ?'

'Um,' said Vince.

I wrote: *WAR – HUNGARY*.

Vince smiled with relief, 'We remember the war, Sir, when we were very hungry.'

He's blown it! I thought. Now Mr Mackington knew he was lying, and we'd both spend the rest of our lives in detention.

Mr Mackington smiled with his mouth, though his steely eyes were still busy inquisiting. He said gently, 'Well, Vince, I look forward to seeing your poem next week. I'm sure it's going to be very imaginative.'

'Oh, for sure, Sir,' sighed Vince, 'for sure!'

'Right, who'd like to go next?' asked Mr Mackington.

Nathan Lumsdyke's hand shot into the air like a Zoggian stink missile and waved desperately. 'Sir, I've actually done an excellent poem, Sir. It's actually a sonnet, Sir, written in the style of Shakespeare actually.'

'Ah yes, Shakespeare,' said Mr Mackington, 'the greatest writer of love poems in the history of the English language. We'd love to hear your sonnet, Mr Lumsdyke.'

'*Shall I compare thee to a starry night?*' read Nathan in what he imagined was his most expressive voice, '*Thy beauty, like the moon, but twice as bright . . .*'

As Nathan's Shakespeare-style poem droned on, Vince gave me a thumbs up. I gave him one back, and scratched my itchy nose. Something odd was going on here. I knew Mr Mackington didn't believe Vince's excuse, so why had he let him off?

'Hey, thanks heaps, Brian,' said Vince at lunchtime. 'That Ethnic Excuse was ace, and now I'll be able to use it on Alfa Romeo Day every year! Thanks for writing it.' He punched my upper arm. It was starting to get really sore.

A shadow blotted out the sun and the tall figure of Sean Peters loomed over us. 'Hey Brian, did *you* write that excuse note about Italy?'

'That's right, Sean,' I said modestly.

'It was great, Brian!'

'Thanks, Sean.'

'Really creative, Brian!'

'Thanks, Sean.'

'You've got a top imagination, Brian. That was a real good poem you wrote too, Brian, you know, the one about how your gran was beautiful ...'

'What do you want, Sean?'

'Brian, do you reckon you could think up an excuse for me too? 'Cause I accidentally forgot to study for my science test. But I figure if I could get off school for a couple of hours, Ms Frankton would have held the test by the time I got back. I reckon you could do a really good excuse note, Brian, 'cause that one you did for Vince was brilliant, man ...'

Maybe my Ethnic Excuse really *had* been brilliant, and it would be interesting to see if I could be that clever again. Besides, it was nice that my friends thought I was a genius. Flattery would get you everywhere with Brian Hobble.

'All right, Sean,' I said, 'how about a Medical Excuse? Teachers have to let you off if you've got some bad medical condition.'

'Yeah, but I don't have any bad medical conditions,' said Sean. 'Except when I was in Year Three I broke my collarbone, and before that I had German measles, or rubella – that's its proper name – so I have an immunity to that now, and I got inoculated for measles and whooping cough and mumps ...'

I took out my notebook and wrote:

Dear Ms Frankton,

Please excuse Sean from today's test. He has an appointment with his psychologist to treat his loquacititis (a brain disease that gives him a verbal inability to keep his mouth shut).

Signed, Mr Peters

This was clever. Ms Frankton was weird enough to believe anything, and teachers were supposed to go easy on kids with rare brain disorders.

'I do talk a lot, don't I?' said Sean, when he'd read my note.

'Some people have commented on it from time to time,' I said.

Sean grinned. 'Then that's a fantastic excuse, Brian!'

'Thanks, Sean.'

'You're awesome, Brian!'

'I know I am, Sean.'

'I'll just hide out in the toilets till the class is nearly over, then come in out of breath, like I've run all the way from the psychologist's, and I'm real disappointed I missed the test. Drama's good for teaching you how to act things like that, isn't it, Brian?'

'Sure is, Sean.'

'Thanks, Brian, you're a pal. Now, there's one other thing I reckon you could write for me. It's not an excuse note this time, but it needs a great writer like you to do it, Brian ...'

'Go away, Sean.'

'Okay, Brian.' He went away.

Another little problem solved! Maybe I really did have a clever second brain. When Graham grew his new brain in the *Think Twice* book, he was able to rob banks by hacking into top secret computer systems. It was Graham's bad luck that when the cops caught up with him, his brilliant brain had gone off on an overseas holiday, leaving him to go to court without it.

I hoped my genius brain wouldn't desert me just now. I might need its help to get me through our next lesson. My least favourite subject in the whole world – P.E.

physical education *n. fi-zik-ul ed-yew-kay-shun.* Taking something which should be fun (i.e. playing games) and using it to cause total misery by making it a compulsory school subject.

I love playing sport, but I've always hated P.E. The letters ought to stand for 'Painful Embarrassment' instead of Physical Education. The cross-country runs we did in P.E. left me wheezing for my asthma puffer. Then our sports teacher, Mr Quale, would make us do push-ups and pull-ups and stretching exercises devised in ancient dungeons. But today's lesson was sure to be the worst P.E. class I'd ever had in my entire life. Because the Garunga School Support Committee had generously raised funds to give Mr Quale a new instrument of torture – an indoor rock-climbing wall.

Mrs Davenport unveiled the climbing wall at a special ceremony last Saturday and now we were going to be the first class to use it.

Two sides of the gym were covered with plywood, dotted with bizarre plastic handholds in various shapes and colours. The climbing wall towered over us, angling into an evil bulge in the corner and spreading out across the ceiling. With its dangling ropes and wicked metal hooks, it looked like a medieval rack, only going straight up. It would have fitted perfectly into the chapter in *Escape from Planet Zog* where the inquisitors hung Captain Loopy upside down by his toenails.

Mr Quale growled at us in a voice exactly like a Zoggian guard's: 'Rock climbing is dangerous! Rock climbers fall. Rock climbers get killed.' Oh, really? I thought. Funny that he hadn't mentioned that in his speech to the parents at the opening ceremony.

'But rock climbing is also fun,' said Mr Quale. 'It gives you a chance to test yourself. Do it sensibly, and it's as safe as walking up your grandma's driveway.' Mr Quale had obviously never walked up my grandma's driveway, and he certainly hadn't seen Grandma backing the car along it. 'Look after your climbing partner, and look after your equipment, and nobody will get hurt.'

Then he told us gory stories about accidents. The boy whose palms burned off when he tried to grab a fast-moving rope, the girl who fell so hard that her leg bones were forced out through the soles of her feet ... I was sure these things would soon be happening to me too. Only the sweat pouring from my palms would probably put out any fire before it burned them, and I was feeling so weak I didn't have any bones in my legs. Anything to do with heights and climbing totally terrified me.

I glanced around the class. Non-sporty kids, among them Cassie Wyman and Nathan Lumsdyke, were looking like Captain Loopy's crew being taken into the inquisition chamber and wondering who'd be the first to crack under torture.

'Pay attention, you snivelling slugs,' said Mr

Quale. 'What I'm going to teach you now may save your miserable little lives.'

He went on to demonstrate the climbing safety equipment. For a perfectly safe sport where nobody was going to get hurt, there sure was a lot of it. There were padded harnesses which went around your waist and thighs. There were woven nylon ropes which Mr Quale said would take a weight of several tonnes. 'That's even enough to catch you when you fall, Incredible Bulk,' he said, pointing to our class giant, Arthur Neerlander. There were bolts and aluminium carabiners and belaying devices which clipped and screwed and snapped open and shut. The gear was all brand spanking, sparkling new. No blood on it yet.

ROCK Climbing Tip #1

"Don't climb with a partner who is heavier than you."

We chose climbing partners. Vince and I picked each other. Kelvin Moray chose Rocco Ferris. Sean Peters was paired up with Bulk Neerlander. Abby and Sofie and Sarah, the three girls who did everything together, started an argument about who'd have to miss out and go with Jody Helmson.

Madeline Chubb was left on her own for a while, which wasn't surprising. When your life may depend on your partner's level head and quick thinking, nobody wants to be stuck with a total Coco Pop like Madeline. Cassie Wyman stepped over to join her. Cassie was that kind of girl. It was the reason I was in love with her. That and her being totally cute.

Next we practised strapping on the harnesses and locking the belay devices. We tested the ropes which snaked down from pulleys in the ceiling and felt how they stretched to give a soft jolt as we bounced in our harnesses. Arthur Neerlander climbed a few holds up the wall and jumped off, dropping his massive weight into the harness. Sean, hooked to Arthur's rope, was whipped feet first into the air as Arthur thumped into the floor.

'Hey!' called Mr Quale. 'You try tricks like that again, Sonny Jim, and I'll rip out your intestines and use them for a bungee rope!'

I nervously leaned my weight into my harness. Vince was belaying me, and he was only just strong enough to take my weight. But with the rope bolted to the floor behind him, he managed it all right.

When we'd all had a turn at belaying and being belayed, Mr Quale called, 'That'll do, thrill-seekers. Now let's see how far up this route you little monkeys can get.'

One by one we tried to climb to the top of the wall, using the numbered blue plastic holds, which Mr Quale said were the easiest.

There were a few surprises. The best climbers were not the people you'd expect to be good at it. Kelvin Moray thought he was so fantastic at sport, but after he'd reached hold 7, his foot slipped off and he was immediately dangling on the rope. Rocco Ferris and Vince made it to holds 9 and 10 before giving up. Sean Peters was a bit of a star. I'd never thought Sean would be good at anything except talking. But his long spider monkey arms reached out and he made it to hold 13, nearly all the way to the top.

Next was Jody Helmson. She was the smallest girl in our class, and mostly famous for her weak stomach. She threw up during every yucky science class. It was wise not to sit near her on a school bus trip, especially when the bus was winding round lots of corners. Jody had brought special shoes for this P.E. lesson, tiny little rubber ones you'd think a five-year-old wouldn't squeeze into. She slipped them on and hobbled across to the wall. She stuck her fingers into a little bag on her harness and rubbed white chalky stuff on her hands. Then she climbed.

It was amazing. She didn't seem to hurry. She just slid up the wall on her matchstick arms. It was as if she weighed nothing – like a tiny yellow and brown bug.

'Way to go, Jody!' breathed Sean Peters, nudging me in the ribs. 'She's hot, isn't she, Brian? Isn't it interesting how girls' bottoms look different when they're hanging in the air and you're looking up at them?'

I was still worrying about what I'd look like when I had to climb myself, so I hadn't noticed this strange phenomenon. Although now Sean had pointed it out, the bottom above us did look quite impressive.

Jody passed holds 9 and 10, then paused for a moment. The next hold was out of reach. Her arms were way too short. She rocked back a couple of times, then jumped, catching hold 11 with her left hand and immediately grabbing 12. She scrambled up past 13, 14 and 15 to slap the top of the wall, and Abby Post lowered her down again.

'Hey, Jody Helmson! Half girl, half gecko!' grinned Mr Quale, clapping. 'You've played this game before.'

Jody shrugged. 'My brother does climbing at Uni. He's taken me up to the mountains a few times.'

I was sure I wouldn't get anywhere near the top. Part of me didn't want to anyway. The horrible thing about climbing is, the higher you go, the further you have to fall. I took a quick suck on my asthma puffer. It was my turn.

'Okay,' called Mr Quale. 'Who is this next young man, his face so pale and drained of all expression? It's Brian Hobble, who can slide up a wall like a slug up the side of a beer glass. Show us what you can do, Brian!'

Cassie Wyman gave me a smile, but a sort of strained one. She was the world's most unsporty person and I was sure she wasn't looking forward to her turn.

Deep breath in, deep breath out. Go!

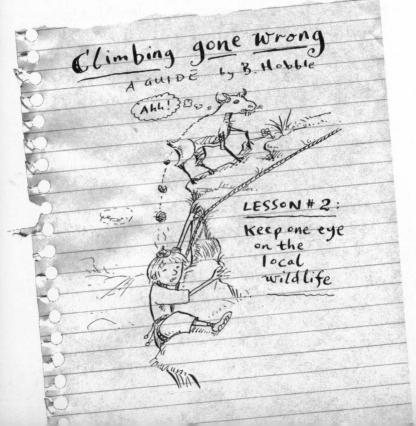

Climbing gone wrong
A GUIDE by B. Hobble

Ahh!

LESSON # 2:
Keep one eye on the local wildlife

The first handholds were big rounded cups, with room to curl my fingers into them. I pulled my feet on to the footholds below them, and flattened the side of my face against the wall. Vince took up the slack on the rope. A heave of my right leg and I could reach the next hold. 'Beauty, Brian,' called Vince. 'Go for the left one now.'

I prised my left hand off the cup hold and reached for the next knob of blue plastic. Whoops! My body swung away from the wall. I grabbed for the cup hold again, and hung on, my cramped arms shaking under the strain. 'Derrr!' said Kelvin Moray.

I had to do better than this. Even Madeline Chubb had made it further up the wall than I had. I needed a suck on my asthma puffer, but it was deep in my pocket and I didn't dare let go of the holds to reach for it. I would have needed a third arm to pull it out.

Below me, other kids started calling advice. 'It's easy, Brian,' came Sean Peters' voice. 'Get your foot up onto 3 and your left hand on 5, then you can pull yourself up to hold 7.' 'Go on, Brian.' 'Just reach up with your right hand, Brian.' 'Anyone can do it, Brian . . .'

'Let him work it out himself, people,' said Mr Quale. 'He's just thinking about it. Brian Hobble's the Ice Man, cool as a frozen icy pole.'

He was half right. I wasn't cool, but I was frozen. My legs had no power left in them, and my bent

47

arms were shaking uncontrollably. I pressed my face into the wood of the wall and tilted my head upwards. I had to get out of this. Hold 7 beckoned.

The trickle of advice from the gym floor had become a flash flood, mixed with jeers from the Kelvin Moray gang. 'Go on, Brian!' 'What's the matter, Brian?' 'Scared, are you Brian?' 'He doesn't climb like a gecko, he climbs like a hippo!'

This was getting to the total, utter, mortifying embarrassment stage. I glanced down and caught Cassie's eye. She was one of the few kids not heckling or offering advice. She must have been thinking about how she'd soon be hanging up on the wall, suffering the way I was suffering now.

Amazingly, my brand new brain suggested a brilliant idea. 'Brian Hobble,' hissed my brain, 'you're an actor now. Use your power! Remember that mime lesson – make the invisible seem *real*!' At once I knew what I had to do.

'Oh you brute! I'll get you!' I yelled. I slapped at the wood under hold 7, then pushed off the wall and hung in the harness. I swung back towards the wall, slapping frantically. Vince took my weight and lowered me down.

'What's wrong, Ice Man?' asked Mr Quale.

'There's a spider up there, on hold 7, Sir. With this wicked orange stripe on his back, Sir. One of the real poisonous kind. A single bite and they can paralyse you, Sir.'

'Oh yeah, as if!' sneered Kelvin Moray.

'Are you sure, Brian?' asked Mr Quale.

'I only saw him for a moment, then he crawled into a crack in the wall,' I said. 'I did what I could to scare him away.'

'I'll get him, Sir,' said Sean Peters, climbing up a few holds.

'No, come down, Seven Eleven,' said Mr Quale. 'If there's a nest of spiders in there, we'll have to close the wall and get the pest guys to come and exterminate them.' He called everyone in. 'Sorry about this, folks, but safety has to be a priority. Brian found a dangerous spider on the wall, and we can't risk using it again until it's been checked out.'

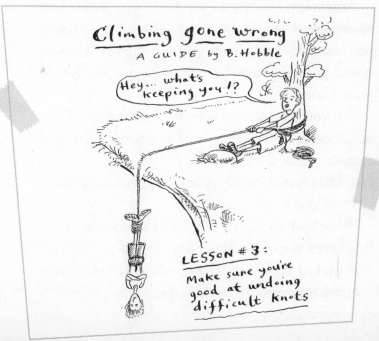

There were a lot of groans, but I noticed that Cassie and a few others were looking more relaxed than they had been a few minutes ago. 'I know it's disappointing,' said Mr Quale, 'but I'll get on to it straight away and we'll have the wall ready for more thrilling action as soon as possible. In fact, next time we should have a Human Fly Championship to find the best climber in the class.'

So ended our first lesson on the Wall of Death. As we went back to the change rooms people looked at me strangely. I knew I wasn't the only person who was pleased that climbing had finished early, but nobody was coming forward to thank me.

Only my brilliant brain would talk to me. 'See, I can get you out of anything, Brian!' it whispered. 'If it wasn't for me, you'd still be stuck on that wall with everyone laughing at you. Now you've not only saved yourself from embarrassment, but you've saved Cassie too.'

'It's just a temporary let off,' I muttered. 'What happens when Mr Quale gets us back on the wall again?'

'I'll think of something,' said my brilliant brain.

'Promise?'

'Trust me,' said my brain. 'You're a genius now, Brian. Get used to it. Enjoy the feeling.'

I tried to enjoy the feeling, only I couldn't concentrate. My nose was itching like crazy.

shemozzle n. shee-mo-zul. A scheme that seems okay at first, but which turns out to be a complete and utter disaster. (See also **debacle**, **chaos**, **catastrophe**, **disorder**, **total stuff-up**.)

A few days later my awesome new brain turned out to be very useful indeed. A clever brain was just what I needed as I tackled my next spine-chilling, gut-churning assignment: preparing for my DAGS audition.

I couldn't find the right speech in Elly Gerballo's *Try Out* book. I wanted something which would show Cassie and Vince and Sean and everyone else at DAGS that I was a real cool dude, who should get the part of a hero in the play.

None of the speeches in the book was about cool dude heroes. There was a sad clown telling why he'd been kicked out of the circus, a girl looking forward to her first date, a Shakespeare speech I didn't understand, and a little kid crying because he'd lost his mother in a supermarket. I couldn't see myself acting any of those parts. I was stuck.

Then the night before the audition, my super-genius brain tapped me on the shoulder. 'Be daring,

Brian,' it said, 'be original. Make up your own audition piece.'

'What???' said my mouth.

'You're a great writer, Brian,' whispered my brain. 'Drama is about being creative. No one else in that DAGS group would think of anything as clever as inventing their own speech.'

'I'll try,' said my mouth.

I took a pen and paper and sat at my desk. Deep breath in, deep breath out. What sort of part would I be good at playing? A star footballer? A pop idol? A superhero maybe, with amazing supernatural powers?

'You can be anyone you like, Brian,' said my brain, nudging me in the ribs. 'That's what's so great about drama – you can be better than you are in real life. Like, in real life you might be a pathetic little schoolkid who can't reach hold 7 on a stupid climbing wall, but on stage you can be totally cool and in control.'

'And funny too,' muttered my mouth, 'like Captain Loopy in *Escape from Planet Zog*.' A smile curled out of the corner of my mouth as I took my copy off the shelf. Because now I'd had a truly fantastic idea! I started to write ...

Ladies and Gentlemen, this is Captain Loopy speaking. Our spaceship will shortly be landing on Planet Zog ...

Half an hour later, lying in front of me was the most amazing drama audition piece anyone had written since the Big Bang. It was brilliant! Nobody else would think of anything like this. I'd written a speech like Captain Loopy would make, using bits of the story from the book.

Ladies and Gentlemen, this is Captain Loopy speaking. Our spaceship will shortly be landing on Planet Zog. Please ensure that your seat is upright and the clothes peg on your nose is securely fastened. The weather for our arrival is cloudy with eruptions of brown gas ... Uh-oh, what's this? Alien Death Fighter approaching from the port bow. Crew, prepare the fart gun defences! Activate the anti-slime shield! ...

When she saw how brilliantly I acted Captain Loopy, Elly Gerballo would have to give me the starring role in Lancelot Cummins' new play. No more puny, pathetic, uncool Brian Hobble. Now I'd be a superhero!

I set up my bedroom as Captain Loopy's spaceship. I practised the speech over and over until I knew it word perfect. I thought up actions, and rehearsed miming the battle where Captain Loopy wrestles the foul little Zoggian alien who sneaks into the control deck. My scene ended with Captain Loopy kissing the beautiful Lena Galaxa. Of course I'd be acting the scene on my own, so I had to mime an imaginary Lena. It felt a bit clunky and awkward.

In the broom cupboard I found a mop, and stuffed in a kitchen drawer was the silver wig Mum had worn to her office Christmas party. I draped the wig over the end of the mop and pretended that it was Lena for the kissing part, being careful not make actual lip-to-mop contact of course.

'I told you we could do it, Brian!' said my fantastic brain. 'The scene with you kissing a mop will be hilarious, and those other DAGS will be blown away by your brilliance.'

———————— ♡ ————————

We sat on the gym mats and watched as one by one, DAGS kids stepped up to the front to perform their audition pieces. At the back, Lancelot Cummins and Elly Gerballo perched on plastic chairs, whispering, smiling and passing each other notes.

This was scary stuff. In a few minutes everyone would be able to judge what I was like at acting. I took a puff on the asthma inhaler to clear the aliens out of my chest. I was sure the kids around me must be able to hear my heart thumping. I nervously

adjusted the silver wig on my Lena Galaxa mop, and waited my turn.

But as the auditions went on, I became more and more convinced my Captain Loopy scene was going to be a knockout. Most other kids were very nervous, and nobody else had dared write their own speech. Leeanne, Sioux and Vince clutched the *Try Out* book with shaky hands and stumbled through their lines with wobbly voices. Sean Peters read the sad clown speech, but instead of saying 'I edged the egg towards Edward the Elegant Elephant', he said, 'I egged the edge towards Elward the Edegant Egelant.' He tried three times and still couldn't get it right.

I sat back and watched them come and go, like a

champion time trial cyclist who waits for all the others to ride first, knowing that when his turn comes he'll coolly blast them away with a world record. My Captain Loopy audition piece was sure to be the best, the most dramatic and easily the most original.

The only other actor who was any good at all was Cassie Wyman. She played a migrant girl who's just got off the plane in New York, and whose fiancé is supposed to meet her. She knew the speech off by heart, and had even brought an overcoat as a cos-tume and a suitcase to use as a prop. I kind of choked up watching her, and when we realised the migrant girl's fiancé wasn't going to turn up, every-one wanted to take her home themselves.

'Terrific, Cassie,' breathed Elly.

'Lovely,' added Lance Cummins.

Madeline Chubb didn't do a speech. She stood in front of us and didn't say anything. She just blew out her cheeks, flapped her hands beside her face, and opened and shut her mouth, stopping occasionally to bump into mimed walls.

'Hey, great work Madeli,' said Elly. 'Am I right in thinking that was an abstract representation of the frustration of someone trapped in a surreal prison?'

'Not really,' shrugged Madeline, 'I was being a goldfish.' Boy, Madeline Chubb was weird!

'Well, it was a very interesting piece, Madeli,' said Elly. 'Who's next?'

Nathan Lumsdyke's hand shot up. Nathan's hand had been shooting up after every person finished, but now you'd think he was busting to go to the toilet he was so desperate.

'Miss, can I go next, please, Miss? My piece is actually excellent.' I knew exactly which speech Nathan would choose. He thought he was so intellectually superior he'd be sure to do the Shakespeare one from the *Try Out* book.

As Nathan carefully positioned a plastic chair in the middle of the acting space, I cast my admiring eye over my wonderfully original, inventive audition piece. I was so pleased I'd be doing something that nobody else could have thought up. Then Nathan started his speech. It wasn't the Shakespeare one. Instead he said, 'Ladies and Gentlemen, this is Captain Loopy speaking. We will shortly be landing on Planet Zog ...'

It was incredible! It was shocking! Nathan performed a long audition piece adapted from Lancelot Cummins' book, and it was exactly like mine! He did the same bit with the Zoggian Death Fighters attacking. When the oxygen supply was cut off, he mimed Captain Loopy holding his breath, just like I was going to do. He wrestled the little alien. Worse, when it came to kissing Lena Galaxa, he took Cassie Wyman by the hand, pulled her up on stage, and kissed her! Worst of all, she kissed him back, while everybody clapped.

The audience loved it. All the DAGS, and even Elly and Lance Cummins were laughing. Cassie Wyman went back to her place and rolled back on the floor, giggling. I'd never seen her in such hysterics. As Nathan bowed and sat down on the mat again, everyone burst into huge applause. 'Nathan, that was just fabulous,' called Elly, wiping the tears out of her eyes. 'Who's left? Oh yes, Brian Hobble.'

What could I do? No way could I do the same thing Nathan had just done. Everyone would think I'd just copied him. I struggled awkwardly to my feet, clutching my mop and the silver wig, cursing my new genius brain that had got me into this total mess.

'You said this would be good!' I hissed to my brain. 'You said everyone would be blown away by my brilliance! You said ...' My brain muttered some excuse about being late for an important business meeting, then climbed out the window and ran away down the street. I was on my own.

Everyone was looking at me. Lancelot Cummins, my friends Vince and Sean. Nathan. And worst of all, Cassie. 'Relax, Brian,' said Elly, 'Take your time to get settled. What piece are you going to do for us?'

My mouth opened and shut, but nothing came out. Now everyone would think I was copying Madeline Chubb's goldfish mime. I had to say something, but I hadn't learned any other audition piece. I couldn't even read anything because I didn't have the *Try Out* book in my hand.

I looked at my silver-wig mop girl, my mouth opened again, and out came the poem I'd written for English:

'Your beautiful eyes, as you move with such grace
Your beautiful hair frames your beautiful face,
The beautifullest thing that I've seen for a while
Is your beautiful smile.'

My poem had sounded bad when I read it in class, and it sounded even worse at DAGS. When it finished, I saw that everyone was still watching me. They expected more. The poem on its own was too short. My genius brain had left my mouth to make something up, which had often got me into trouble in the past. My mouth babbled on . . .

'Let me walk beside you,
take your hand along the shore
Let me live beside you, be mine for evermore
Will you be my turtle dove
Will you be my sweetest love . . .'

It needed more action, something to distract from the appalling awfulness of the slushy words, which were gushing out of my mouth and slopping into the Drama room. I lifted my arms high to the heavens, then fell to my knees, and clasped the silver wig mop up above me, like I was proposing to an imaginary girl, and gabbled some more . . .

'Take me to the twinkling stars,
Is that Venus? Is that Mars?
Let me overflow with joy,

Say I am your special boy.
You excite me, you can please me,
Love me, hold me, take me, squeeze me ...!'

When I ran out of lines to say, I faltered to a stop. I couldn't think of anything else to do, so I propped the mop against a chair and shuffled off stage. It must have looked as though in spite of all the loving things I'd said, the girl had turned me down. I wasn't the cool hero after all. I was pathetic little Brian Hobble who'd been knocked back by a mop in a silver wig!

If you did something like this in a normal classroom, you'd never live it down. There'd be so much 'derr'-ing from kids like Kelvin Moray, you'd have to change schools and move house and get a new name and have a plastic surgeon give you a new face.

But at DAGS things were different. There was a pause. I didn't dare catch anybody's eye, but I thought I heard Madeline Chubb sniffle. Then there was a round of applause as I sat down next to Vince. Leeanne whispered something to Julie, who nodded wisely. The DAGS thought I was cool!

'Great piece, Brian,' said Elly. 'Where did you find it?'

'I just made it up,' I said.

'Wow,' said Elly.

'Brian Hobble and I have met before,' said Lancelot Cummins. 'He's a really outstanding young writer.'

'Wow,' said Elly again.

Cassie Wyman smiled her devastating smile at me. My brilliant brain came back from its meeting just in time to share my moment of glory. 'Didn't I tell you, Brian?' it whispered. 'You were brilliant. Action, comedy, sad bits – you had the lot!'

I stared modestly at the ground as Lancelot Cummins stepped awkwardly over people sitting on the mats and made his way out to the front. 'Well done everyone,' he said. 'I'm really impressed with what I've seen, and I'm sure we'll find terrific actors for all the parts. Just one small point though – *Cyberno*'s about an army of soldiers going off to war. Now there's no problem with girls playing space fighters too, but it would be good to have a few more people in this show, especially boys. If we've only got five space fighters battling a handful of aliens, it's going to seem like a very little war!'

'There you are, fellas,' said Elly. 'If you can talk your mates into coming along, do that. And girls, bring your boyfriends. The more the merrier!'

'Brian will find some boys,' said Cassie Wyman. 'He's been good at getting them along before.' She flashed me *that* smile again. Something melted in my lower stomach, like when Captain Loopy's deputy Andrew the Android turns things into pools of plasma with his laser-like gaze.

'No problem,' I grinned. 'How many do you want?'

If Cassie wanted me to get more boys to DAGS, I'd get them. Although I had no idea how. The only friends I had any influence over were Vince and Sean, and they were already signed-up DAGS.

'Brian, don't worry about it,' said my brilliant brain. 'A genius makes his own luck, so things will just keep on getting better. Something's sure to turn up.'

AMAZINGLY, my brain was absolutely right. Something turned up straight away. That night the phone rang in the Hobble house.

'I'll get it,' squeaked my little brother Matthew. He always dashed to pick up the phone first and sometimes got involved in long conversations with people doing consumer surveys and telemarketing. Once he signed up for a gold credit card before the person ringing found out he was only five. This time it wasn't telemarketing.

'Briiiiii-an!' called Matthew. 'Kelvin Moray wants to talk to you.' Kelvin Moray? He'd never rung me before in his entire life. What could my worst enemy possibly have to say to me?

I took the phone from Matthew. 'This is Brian Hobble's residence, how can I help you?' I said, using the icy-cold phone voice Mum puts on when someone's trying to sell her a vacuum cleaner.

63

'You're a liar, Brian,' said Kelvin Moray.

'I'm a what?' I said. Somehow the temperature in our house had risen 20,000 degrees and I was worried that even down the phone line Kelvin might notice the blood rushing into my guilty cheeks.

'You're a very good liar, Brian,' said Kelvin. 'People believe you when you tell a lie.'

'Perhaps you could explain to me what this is all about?' I said.

'I need to talk to you, Brian.'

'I don't need to talk to you, Kelvin,' I said.

'I need you to help me, Brian.'

Kelvin Moray was a thug and a bully. If he really needed my help, he'd have to get down on his knees and beg. I kept my voice level, cool and controlled: 'Could you perhaps give me a good reason why I should help you, Kelvin?'

'Because.'

'Because what?'

This was becoming one of those really stupid conversations. I would have hung up, only I was curious to know what we were talking about.

'Mr Quale caught me on the climbing wall this afternoon,' said Kelvin. 'It's officially out of bounds till it's been fumigated against spiders. But there aren't any spiders, are there Brian?'

I wasn't going to answer that.

I just ever so slightly raised one inscrutable evil genius eyebrow. I did it really well, and it was a shame Kelvin couldn't see it through the phone line.

'I got banned from climbing, Brian, and tomorrow I have to go and explain to Mrs Davenport why I was on the wall without permission.'

'Oh.'

'With my parents.'

I couldn't imagine anything worse than being sent to see our school principal with my parents. My brain thought, *Serves you right, Kelvin. I hope you get grounded for a trillion years!* My mouth said, 'Oh dear me, this world is so unjust, Kelvin! I hope you don't get into *too* much trouble!'

Kelvin poked his finger into my chest. Of course, he couldn't really poke a finger through the phone, but he talked like he was poking a finger. 'Vince Peretti reckons you're real good at thinking up excuses, Brian. So write me an excuse, write it now, and write it good.'

'And the reason I should do this is …?'

'If you don't, I'll bash you,' snarled Kelvin.

That sounded like a pretty good reason. I'd seen kids bashed by Kelvin Moray and I didn't want to be next on his list. 'Not good enough,' I said. I was feeling very brave now, and my new brain had just made another brilliant suggestion. 'If you want me to write you an excuse note, Kelvin, you have to join DAGS.'

'No way!'

'Sorry, no note then,' I said.

In the background, I heard a man's voice snarling, 'Off the phone, son. Quick smart. Or you'll get a good hiding!' Kelvin Moray sure had a charming family. You could see where he got his lovely personality from.

'All right, Brian, email the excuse to moray.k@bignet.com,' said Kelvin quickly. 'If it gets me out of trouble with Mrs Davenport, I'll come to DAGS.'

'It's a deal.'

'Do it tonight,' said Kelvin.

'Consider it done and don't even bother to thank me, Kelvin.'

Kelvin didn't thank me. The phone just went dead.

'Got him!' said my brilliant brain. This was an amazing win/win opportunity. I'd write Kelvin an excuse note. If Mrs Davenport didn't believe it, Kelvin would be in big trouble. If she did believe it, I'd get one of the toughest kids in school to come to DAGS. Cassie would be so impressed. What's more, I'd love to see the great Kelvin Moray hanging round DAGS for the next few weeks, playing some boring little part like a Zoggian space slug.

My brain had already thought up a fiendishly, devilishly clever excuse note for Kelvin. I typed it on Mum's computer:

Dear Mrs Davenport,

Mr and Mrs Moray will be unable to attend tomorrow's meeting to discuss Kelvin's behaviour. They are both spies working on a top secret assignment and will be out chasing enemy agents tomorrow.

Kelvin is a spy too. He is one of our bravest and most brilliant agents and only pretends to be a bit stupid sometimes so his cover won't be blown. He needs to practise climbing spider-infested walls for the dangerous mission he has to do in the school holidays, scaling cliffs in the Amazon jungle.

Signed,
K.G. Spivakov
Director, Office of National Security

P.S. Do not tell anyone about this message (especially the Amazon jungle part) and don't phone Mr and Mrs Moray to see if this message is real. That would endanger their secret assignment ... and their lives. Just give the message to Kelvin and he will pass it on.

I could hardly stop laughing my wicked warlord laugh as I scratched my nose and emailed the message. Even Professor Mucus had never thought up a scheme as clever as this one.

The phone rang, and I checked my watch. Not even two minutes. I picked up the phone and said, 'Hobble residence. Your call may be monitored for security purposes.'

'Do you really think Mrs Davenport will believe I'm a spy?' hissed Kelvin.

'Why not?' I said. 'You're so cool and confident and good at sport. If anyone in our school was a secret agent it would be you.'

'Cool!' said Kelvin, and hung up.

What an evil genius I was! When Mrs Davenport read that note, Kelvin would be in more trouble than Captain Loopy when the Zoggians buried him up to his nostrils in a tank of brown you-know-what, then turned on the wave-making machine.

On the other hand, there was just the tiniest remote possibility that Mrs Davenport would believe my excuse. Other teachers had accepted the excuses I'd written for Vince and Sean. If Mrs Davenport did swallow it, DAGS would get a new cast member. Either way, I'd be a winner.

'Thank you, oh my brilliant brain,' I murmured.

'Any time,' my brain whispered back.

I scratched my itchy nose again. It was getting annoying, the way my nose itched whenever I was being brilliant. Maybe mosquitoes were attracted to intelligence. Perhaps a mozzie had bitten me on the nose to suck out my blood, because my DNA would make him intelligent too … No, that was too ridiculous to even think about!

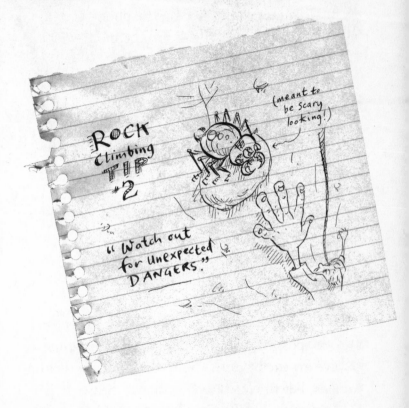

typecasting *n. typ-kar-sting.* Where they give actors parts that are just like the people are in real life, like making a bully play the bad guy, and a complete idiot play a complete idiot.

NEXT morning started with a disaster. I suppose I should have seen it coming, but it still gave me a real punch in the guts. Or maybe even just below the guts, where punches really hurt.

The disaster didn't look like a disaster from a distance. It was just an innocent-looking sheet of paper, pinned on the DAGS noticeboard. It was only when I got up close to it that I realised how totally, utterly, completely and unmitigatedly disastrous this disaster was:

CYBERNO
by Lancelot Cummins

CAST LIST

CAPTAIN LOOPY, space commander

Nathan Lumsdyke

LENA GALAXA, a pretty technician

Cassandra Wyman

SPACE FIGHTERS

Sioux Branson

Anna Reys

Leeanne Groves

Kaytlyn O'Day

Jennifer Chang

Laura MacLyntock

ALIENS

Vincent Peretti

Madeline Chubb

Ami Farouk

Julie Salter

Emily Lupos

CHRIS, a young space cadet

Sean Peters

CYBERNO, a poet

Brian Hobble

NEW DAGS ARE ALWAYS WELCOME.
WE HAVE PARTS FOR EVERYONE!!!!

This was terrible! After that disgusting sneaky trick he pulled in the auditions, Nathan Lumsdyke was bound to get the part of Captain Loopy, but what about Cassie Wyman being his co-star Lena Galaxa????!!! What if they had to kiss each other all through rehearsals, and then in the performance on stage? How would I be able to bear to watch it?

And my name was last on the cast list, as if I'd only just scraped into the play! It was like those lunchtime football matches where kids line up and the captains pick the teams. The last one chosen is the kid everyone thinks is hopeless. I looked at the notice again. I wasn't playing a cool hero of course, I was playing a poet! What sort of pathetic, wussy lines might I have to say?

At least I wouldn't have to wait long to find out. The next rehearsal was that afternoon. And at that rehearsal, DAGS had a new member. Kelvin Moray sneaked in the back door of the gym, while we were waiting for Elly to arrive. He looked as nervous as he would have been on a spider-infested wall in the Amazon jungle, hanging above a pool of piranhas.

'I'm only coming this one time, Brian,' he muttered. 'Just 'cause you got me out of trouble.'

'So Mrs Davenport *believed* you were a secret agent?'

'Why wouldn't she?' said Kelvin. 'You said yourself I'd be perfect as a spy. Mrs Davenport says now the pest company's got rid of the spiders, I can go on the climbing wall any time.'

'Really?'

'And she's giving me a day off school whenever our national security is threatened.'

'That's great, Kelvin.' This was sort of freaky. Why had Mrs Davenport accepted my ridiculous excuse note? She wasn't stupid. Something strange, maybe even supernatural was going on. I was absolutely, positively, definitely 110% sure. Almost.

Cassie and Nathan Lumsdyke arrived. Together, I was sorry to see. Cassie's face lit up with that wonderful smile, but of course it wasn't aimed at me. 'Kelvin! Welcome to DAGS,' she said. 'I'm so glad we have another boy in the group.'

'I'm only here 'cause of Brian,' grated Kelvin, 'and I'm only staying till . . .'

Cassie turned triumphantly to Nathan. 'See, Nathan, I told you Brian would get more boys along!' Then she did send a smile in my direction. It didn't entirely make my day, but it did improve it just a little.

'Actually I didn't expect you to be actually interested in drama, Kelvin,' said Nathan.

'I'm not,' muttered Kelvin. 'I'm just here today because Brian said –'

'Because I told him how good *Cyberno* was going to be,' I said quickly. I didn't want Cassie to know about my excuse note writing. And I had the great Kelvin Moray in my brilliant power, so I wanted to enjoy the moment while it lasted. 'Kelvin's hoping he might get a small part in the play.'

'Well, good luck,' said Cassie, moving off to where Nathan had put two chairs together and was patting one of them vigorously, indicating that she should sit next to him.

Kelvin grabbed me by my sore arm. 'I never said I'd be in no play, Brian!'

'You *will* try out for the play,' I said calmly.

'Because if you don't, Mrs Davenport will receive another letter from the Office of National Security, about how certain kids at this school are *pretending* to be spies to get out of doing their homework ...'

'All right, Brian,' said Kelvin. He let go of my arm, but I could hear his teeth grinding together. 'This time, you win.'

'I usually do, these days,' I purred.

Elly Gerballo came over to introduce herself. 'Hello, you're a friend of Brian's are you?' she said.

Kelvin shrugged and mumbled something. I couldn't hear what he said, and it was probably good that Elly didn't hear it either. Kelvin was lots of things, but a friend of Brian's wasn't one of them, certainly not today.

Elly said, 'For now, Kelvin, please just read along with the chorus of space fighters. We'll find you a speaking part in the new scenes Lance Cummins is writing.' Kelvin slouched off to an empty chair in the back row, next to Madeline Chubb. He plonked himself onto it and folded his arms, glaring around the room at the other DAGS. I thought Lance should write an angry slimy Zoggian monster into his play. That would be the perfect part for Kelvin.

Lancelot Cummins passed out copies of the opening act of his play. Nathan, with Cassie beside him, read the part of Captain Loopy, announcing the mission to his crew of space fighters. I flicked my eyes over the first few pages. My pathetic poet character didn't have a single line to say in the first scene. In fact, he didn't even appear on stage. Nathan Lumsdyke did most of the talking.

CAPTAIN LOOPY: Men and Women of Planet Earth. We are in dreadful danger. We must soon cross the Galaxy to battle the revolting Zoggians.

FIGHTERS: Hooray!

CAPTAIN LOOPY: The disgusting Zoggians never clean their toilets.

FIGHTERS: Yuck!

CAPTAIN LOOPY: They've covered their entire planet with brown gunk, and now they want to turn our beautiful Planet Earth into an off-shore sewerage farm, to take the overflow waste from the Great Bog of Zog.

FIGHTERS: (TOGETHER) Shame, shame!

CAPTAIN LOOPY: Our mission is to slow the flow!

FIGHTERS: (CHANT) Captain Loopy, we salute you. We're behind you all the way! Into battle we must go! Slow the flow! Slow the flow!

I watched Kelvin while the others read. He sat sourly among the other space fighters, a sort of silent evil presence. When space fighter lines came around, he just mumbled, eyes flicking around to see what everyone else was doing. Madeline Chubb leaned over and pointed to the lines on Kelvin's script, as if she thought he might have lost the place, but he brushed her hand away.

Then as the scene went on Kelvin started to shout his answers with the rest of them, even punching his fist in the air on 'Slow the flow!'

My mind started to drift as Nathan read on and on, but suddenly my ears snapped to attention, because my character Cyberno was mentioned ...

CAPTAIN LOOPY: Where's Cyberno?

SPACE CADET CHRIS: He's, er, fighting a duel, Captain Loopy.

CAPTAIN LOOPY: A duel?

SPACE CADET CHRIS: An alien insulted him, Captain Loopy.

CAPTAIN LOOPY: An alien insulted Cyberno?

SPACE CADET CHRIS: You know what a hot-headed rebel Cyberno is! He's vowed to fight the alien and force him to apologise.

CAPTAIN LOOPY: We can't go into battle against the Zoggians without Cyberno!

```
            He's the greatest space fighter of
            all. Bring him to me immediately!
    FIGHTERS: Yes Sir!


    THE SPACE FIGHTERS ALL SALUTE AND
    RUN OFF.
```

Cyberno was a hot-headed rebel? The greatest space fighter of all? This was sounding a bit better.

'Well done, everyone,' said Elly Gerballo. 'That was a great first read through! Now we go to Scene 2 where the alien and Cyberno are fighting their duel. Vince, you're the alien, and Brian, you're reading Cyberno.'

As we read Scene 2, I started to feel that maybe Cyberno wasn't such a bad part after all. He was a poet, yes, but he certainly wasn't wussy. He was witty and clever and a fantastic space fighter, an expert with a laser lance.

Scene 2 went like this:

```
    ALIEN: (WITH AN EVIL LAUGH) Ha ha,
           Cyberno! You will regret
           challenging a Kragon warrior.
           I will slice your preposterous
           proboscis off your miserable
           face!
    CYBERNO: (COOLLY) Bring it on, you
```

disgusting lump of space scum.
I can take you left-handed. I can
even compose a poem at the same
time.

THEY CLASH LASER LANCES.

You call me rude names,
you disgusting green blob,
You're a planetary poo,
you're a slimy space slob!

CYBERNO FLICKS THE ALIEN'S LANCE
ASIDE.

ALIEN: I happen to be the Galaxy's
laser lance champion. I'll
shorten your prominent
protuberance!

THE ALIEN CHARGES WITH HIS LASER
LANCE, BUT CYBERNO PARRIES THE
BLOW EASILY.

CYBERNO: My laser lance skills,
I've just naturally got 'em
I'll give you a biff
on your alien bottom!

> HE POKES THE ALIEN'S BACKSIDE WITH HIS
> LANCE. ALIEN SQUEALS AND GRABS HIS
> REAR END.

Everyone nearly wet themselves laughing as Vince and I read the scene. It was brilliant the way Cyberno whips the alien's butt and sends him yelping off the stage, begging for mercy. Even Kelvin Moray couldn't 'derr' me for my performance, not without his mates to play up to. He seemed to be enjoying it anyway, watching me with a silly grin on his face.

There were words in the scene that I didn't understand, like 'proboscis' and 'protuberance', but I didn't want to embarrass myself by asking about them, in case everyone else already knew what they meant. I made a mental note to look them up later.

'Super reading, Vince and Brian!' said Elly. 'We'll leave it there because that scene has lots of action in it. Next rehearsal a friend of mine will come along and help you with the fight choreography. Joe's a stuntman and he specialises in martial arts scenes in films.'

Vince gave me a punch on the arm. He liked the idea of working with a stuntman. So did I. Cyberno was turning out to be a great part in a really cool show!

'And remember, we still need more boys to join

How to fight Aliens
A GUIDE To using a LASER LANCE by B. Hobble
No ② "The Gut Buster"

{ It's a bit like skiing... }

the cast,' said Elly. 'Welcome aboard, Kelvin. It's great to have you in the crew.'

'That's okay,' muttered Kelvin. He caught my eye, then quickly looked away.

'I'll have a few more scenes written for the next rehearsal,' said Lance Cummins. 'There should be some fun in them too, because they're love scenes.'

'Woo-ooh!' said Vince and Sean Peters.

'As well as being an adventure story,' said Lance, 'Cyberno is a love story. Our hero Cyberno is in love with the beautiful Lena Galaxa.'

Everyone's eyes turned to me and Cassie. 'Bingo!'

said my brilliant brain. 'I told you this would work, Brian. Not only do you get to play a cool fighter, but you're the hero of the story who gets the girl. And the girl is Cassie Wyman!'

'Of course true love never runs smooth,' Lancelot Cummins went on, 'and Cyberno's got a rival. His best friend Chris loves Lena Galaxa too.'

Chris? That was Sean Peters' space cadet part! Phew! So Cassie wouldn't be kissing Nathan after all, and my guess was that Lena would end up with Cyberno. I couldn't imagine any character played by Sean Peters getting the girl. Maybe my brilliant brain had been right once again – I was going to come out on top in drama too!

As we left the rehearsal, Nathan Lumsdyke showed me a book.

'I actually did some research with Ms Kitto in the library to find the original play *Cyberno*'s based on,' said Nathan. 'It's actually a classic French play, called *Cyrano de Bergerac* by Edmond Rostand and the story is very interesting.'

'Really?' I said. I tried to sound like I wasn't the slightest bit interested in the love story in an old French play. 'Maybe I'll read it when you've finished with it, Nathan.'

'Actually,' he said, 'I've promised Cassie Wyman that she could borrow it next, but I could actually get her to pass it on to you, Brian.'

'Sure, Nathan,' I said. I shrugged slightly, and

examined my fingernails, using my great acting skills to appear super cool. 'No hurry.' I was desperate to read it of course. I wanted to make sure that Cyberno would get together with Lena Galaxa in the end.

writing career *n. ry-ting kar-eer.*
Where you write as a job, but you find
it careering away like an out-of-control
car going downhill with no brakes.

I was on a roll. Everything I tried was working out
brilliantly. It was like the chapter in *Think Twice*
where Graham's new brain invents a super sports car
which goes by itself and never needs steering. But
once you're on a roll, it's very hard to get off.
Especially when your super sports car speeds up to
3000 kilometres an hour and starts going through
red lights.

Kelvin Moray told all his mates about how he got
out of trouble with Mrs Davenport. He boasted
about his new career as a spy and joked about secret
missions he was planning in Timbuktu and Zanzibar.
He told everyone how smart he'd been to get Brian
Hobble to write his excuse note for him.

Word quickly spread among the criminal elements of Garunga District School that whenever
you were in trouble, a Brian Hobble excuse note
would get you out of it. All week, young offenders

were sidling up to me, speaking out of the corner of their mouths, asking me to write excuse notes for them.

'Can you get me out of the swimming carnival, Brian?' asked Arthur Neerlander.

'I need a permission note to leave school at lunchtime,' said Mario Fenton.

'I forgot to do my science experiment,' whispered Rocco Ferris.

Before long, I became a notorious underworld figure. I felt a bit like Skripton, the sinister little Zoggian who lurks in an underground chamber, inventing secret codes for General Klag. People despise Skripton, but they need his brains, so he has a position of power. For a while, I was powerful too.

Everyone who hadn't studied for tests, or hated sport, or who'd arrived late for school came asking me to put the magic Brian Hobble touch to their excuses. Two of the cutest girls in the Senior School asked me to do them notes so they could get a day off school to meet their boyfriends at the video arcade. It was kind of flattering to be in such demand, so when they asked for my talents, I tried my best to deliver the goods.

I wrote notes to get people out of sport, excuses for failing French tests, and permission slips for school excusions to chocolate factories. I invented dozens of reasons for why people were late back after lunch, or had missed assignments.

I invented sick parents and grandparents. Dozens of aunties and uncles passed away and needed Garunga kids to speak at their funerals. In my skilful writer's hands, science projects on weather were struck by lightning or washed down drains in thunderstorms. Kids in Garunga District School suffered from an amazing variety of crippling diseases that stopped them doing homework or got them out of sports events.

Dear Mr Quale,

Arthur can't go in the swimming carnival this week. He is being treated for a rare infectious skin condition and if it gets in the water it might infect other kids.

Signed, Dr Squiggle (Specialist in Skin Diseases)

Kids were constantly arriving late to school because they'd been training for the Olympic equestrian team, or foiling armed bank robbers, or returning escaped cheetahs to the zoo.

Dear Mr Jessop,

Noel's house was destroyed by a local earthquake last night and his history project slipped down the crack in his bedroom floor ...

For some inexplicable reason, the more ridiculous I made the excuses, the more teachers swallowed them.

> Dear Ms Frankton,
> Rocco's science experiment on mould
> growth exploded last night. Sorry
> about the mess in his work book ...

I disguised my handwriting of course, so nobody would know all the notes were written by the same evil genius, but I couldn't believe the teachers could possibly be so stupid as to swallow everything I wrote. I never actually said someone missed a day of school because they'd been taken by aliens, but I had a sneaky feeling that even if I'd written that, it would have been accepted.

> Dear Madame Lebeau,
> Mario might not remember all his
> French verbs in today's test. He has
> amnesia after a bump on the head and
> keeps forgetting stuff ...
> P.S. Please let him off if he forgets to
> give you this note until after the test.

Time after time, kids came up to me to thank me for getting them out of trouble, join DAGS, and ask for my help for the next time. Sure, I had a brand new genius brain, but there was something super weird going on here.

Normally I might have found it all too freaky and stopped using my writing abilities for evil purposes. But I couldn't stop, because my brilliant brain showed me how to turn my new talent to my advantage. At first I got kids to share their lunch with me, or lend me their computer games, and some even paid money. But if you were in really serious trouble, and wanted a top-of-the-range original Brian Hobble excuse note, you had to join DAGS.

How to fight Aliens

A GUIDE TO USING a LASER LANCE by B.Hobble

Nº ③ " The Bottom Prodder "

{ "Eight-Ball in the top pocket ..." }

Lots of kids did. As I wrote more and more excuse notes, more and more kids started turning up. Every rehearsal, we had two or three new DAGS.

The new DAGS were not good kids. These were tough, hardened offenders. The kids who got into the most trouble needed the best excuse notes. So the ones I was able to blackmail into joining DAGS were the low-life bottom-feeders of the school. Kelvin's sidekicks Rocco and Arthur, as well as Mario Fenton, Tangles and Knobbly Knees from our soccer team, they were all there.

Captain Loopy soon had ten space fighters under his command, and the Zoggian army had grown to fifteen. I was pleased to see how the biggest, toughest kids could still look shy and embarrassed when they had to do drama for the first time. New DAGS hovered uncomfortably in the background, hoping not to get picked to do an improvisation or read one of Lancelot Cummins' new scenes. When they were chosen to step into the spotlight and act, they choked and mumbled and reddened. But they kept coming. They improved.

Most surprising of all, they enjoyed it. Elly Gerballo was brilliant at involving everybody, and keeping the rehearsals fun. Before long, tough new DAGS were marching around in lines, playing space fighters, trying really hard to keep in step and taking shouted orders from Nathan Lumsdyke playing Captain Loopy.

Lancelot Cummins wrote a special part for Kelvin Moray. It wasn't a slimy monster; it was Cyberno's sidekick Andrew the Android, and Kelvin was really pleased about it. Andrew was his favourite character in the book, and Kelvin even started going around the school experimenting with a stiff walk and trying out a robotic voice.

Girls like Leeanne and Sioux and even Madeline Chubb started chatting to the big tough boys when there were breaks in the rehearsal. Nobody 'derred' anybody, even when things went wrong in scenes, or someone forgot their lines.

My character Cyberno starts off in the story being a bit like me – too shy to tell Lena Galaxa that he loves her. But in between fighting battles with aliens, Cyberno's always writing poems, which normally would have been really embarrassing to do with everybody watching.

But when Cyberno wrote a secret love letter to Lena Galaxa, and I had to read it out in rehearsals, even Kelvin Moray and his gang went into hysterics. They weren't paying me out. They were laughing at Lancelot Cummins' brilliantly funny lines. Cyberno wrote this fantastic poem, which would be sure to make Lena fall in love with him:

```
Oh Lena Galaxa, you're my love
My little planetary dove
```

> Your eyes like stars,
> Your lips ripe fruit,
> You're sexy in your astro-suit.
>
> When into Outer Space I blast,
> Your arms will ever hold me fast
> Your lovely smile I take with me
> As I sail through the Galaxy.
>
> Whene'er I wish upon a star
> A million light years don't seem far
> I'll have you know, if I should die
> You are my oxygen supply.

Even the toughest DAGS were clapping when I finished. They were all having a great time.

'This is wonderful,' said Elly. 'Mrs Davenport warned me that most Garunga kids thought doing drama was a bit uncool. But that was a super response. Thank you for being in the play, and thanks for being so supportive of your fellow actors.'

As we left the Drama room, Cassie Wyman came up alongside me. 'It's going to be a great show, don't you think, Brian?'

'Yeah, I reckon.'

'At first I thought it was strange that all those new kids joined DAGS. I wasn't sure I'd like them. But they've been very good, don't you think?'

'Yeah, not bad,' I said.

'They're not the kids you'd expect to be interested in drama, are they? Do you know why they came here?'

'No idea, Cassie.'

Cassie smiled one of those gut-melting, heart-dropping-to-the-knees smiles of hers. 'You're just being modest, Brian. Kelvin told me all those boys joined because you invited them.'

'I suppose I must be quite popular,' I shrugged, scratching my nose. It felt bad not to be telling the whole truth to Cassie. She was the one person in the world I really wanted to be honest with. But I thought she wouldn't approve of me writing those excuse notes. And as for blackmailing people into coming to DAGS . . .

A whiff of Gingernut Cream biscuits drifted across the room – a sure sign that Madeline Chubb was about to join us. 'I didn't know you had so many friends, Brian,' she said. 'Normally the only boys who talk to you are Vince and Sean.' Ouch! Madeline Chubb was so honest it could really hurt.

'What do you think of the play, Brian?' asked Cassie.

'I love it,' I said. 'Although . . .'

'Although what?'

'Nothing,' I said, 'I'm just curious about how it's going to end.' I couldn't tell her that although I liked the play and loved my part of Cyberno, there was something about it that was worrying me.

Cyberno was writing these great love letters to Lena, but for some reason he never signed them with his own name. Instead, he let Lena think the letters were coming from his friend, Space Cadet Chris.

If Cyberno was such a cool, confident dude, why was he so shy about telling Lena he loved her? I couldn't understand it. If he didn't hurry up and declare his love in the next few scenes, there could be a terrible mix-up and Lena would end up with Chris by mistake.

It was only a made-up story in a play of course. Lancelot Cummins could fix Cyberno's problem whenever he liked, and I was pretty sure he'd still make Cyberno get the girl in the end. Then something happened in my real life that was eerily close to what was going on in the play.

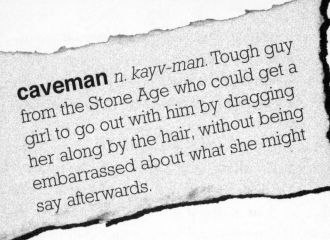

caveman n. kayv-man. Tough guy from the Stone Age who could get a girl to go out with him by dragging her along by the hair, without being embarrassed about what she might say afterwards.

'YOU know why guys like us go for cute chicks, Brian?' asked Sean Peters. 'It's because we're descended from cavemen.'

I kept my mouth shut. Sean Peters often started these really weird conversations, and if you encouraged him by joining in, he'd go on talking forever. Even if you didn't join in, Sean never seemed to notice.

His lecture went on: 'In the Stone Age, cavemen needed cavewomen to collect fruit and berries and have babies. So cavemen chased cavegirls who looked young and healthy. Stone Age women need-ed men who could fight sabre-toothed tigers and hunt woolly mammoths.'

It's lucky for Sean Peters he didn't live in the Stone Age, I thought. He'd never be able to catch even a baby woolly mammoth, so his chances of get-ting a cavegirl would be a big fat zero. Sean's history lesson was moving on: 'So you'd reckon chicks would go for the guys with the biggest muscles, wouldn't you, Brian?'

'Um,' I said, and flexed my skinny arms nervously.

'Wrong!' said Sean. 'Chicks get turned on by guys with big brains.'

'Oh,' I said.

'Cavemen with big brains could discover fire and invent wheels and stuff, so in the end they could look after their women best. It makes sense when you think about it, don't you reckon, Brian?'

'Um,' I said.

'But there was a problem in the Stone Age. How did cavewomen know which cavemen were the brainiest? You know how, Brian?'

I couldn't say 'Um' or 'Oh' again, so I just shrugged.

'Words,' said Sean. 'Even before they had language, cavegirls went for brainy cavemen who could do the nicest grunts. That's why modern chicks go for guys with the smooth chat-up lines. It shows they have big brains and can invent wheels and make fire.'

This was getting too weird. I had to interrupt this conversation or I'd never get to Science on time.

'What's your point here, Sean?'

'Can you write me a love letter, Brian?'

'Write a love letter? To *you*?'

'Not *to* me,' said Sean. '*For* me. You write a letter to this girl I like, and pretend it comes from me.'

95

'You want me to write a love letter to a girl???'

'I got the idea from the play, Brian. You know how I'm sort of nervous about words, like my character Chris.'

'You're great with words, Sean. You could talk under wet concrete.'

'Talk, yeah. Not write. I'm hopeless at writing stuff down, but everyone reckons you're a real good writer, Brian, like Cyberno is. So if you write a real hot letter to this girl, I can pretend it came from me, like Chris does in the play. And then she'll like me.' So Sean Peters liked a girl. 'And she'll want to go out with me,' he added.

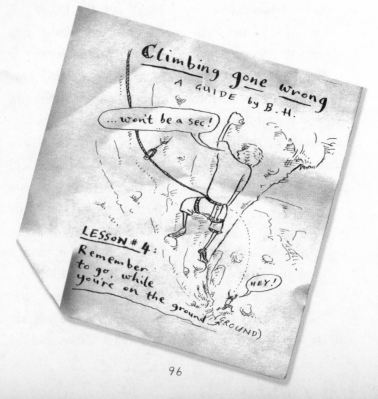

Climbing gone wrong
A GUIDE by B.H.

...won't be a sec!

LESSON # 4:
Remember to go' while you're on the ground (GROUND)

HEY!

'Who is this girl, Seven Eleven?' I asked.

That shut him up. For once the all-night store was on strike.

'Just someone,' he blushed.

'Oh, I see. "Someone,"' I said. You didn't need a genius brain like mine to guess that "someone" was Jody Helmson. We'd seen on the climbing wall how healthy she was. I could imagine Stone Age Sean Peters thinking Jody would be good with the children, and she'd have no problem shinning up a tree when the kids needed more fruit and berries.

'Why don't you just walk up and tell Jo – um, this girl that you like her?' I asked.

'We're just starting out,' he said. 'If I say the wrong thing I might blow it, 'cause you know how sometimes people think I talk too much, so it would be better to write a love letter and give it to her, and like I said, if it's a real good hot letter she'll see I've got good brains and –'

'Okay, I'll do it,' I said.

There were two reasons why I said that:

(1) I wouldn't have to listen to Sean's voice any more.

(2) I wanted the practice. This was my sinister, sneaky, devious, dastardly reason. If Sean's plan worked and my letter made Jody like him, maybe I could write a similar letter to Cassie to tell her how I felt about her. If Jody didn't like the letter and thought Sean was a

complete total idiot, then it would be him getting rejected, not me. This was too perfect!
So out with the writing pad and Brian Hobble was
back in writing genius mode. I really was amazingly
good at this. Three minutes and my masterpiece was
finished. It even rhymed.

My darling, my dear, my precious, my love,
I think you are sweet
as a sweet turtle dove
I think you are hot
as a warm summer breeze
And cool as the grass
that grows under the trees.

'Not bad, Brian,' said Sean. 'Not bad at all. Do you
reckon she'll like it?'

'She'll throw herself at you when she reads this,' I
said. 'Oh, I haven't signed it yet.'

Sean grabbed my arm. 'No, don't sign it. Just
write: "Your Secret Admirer". Then I won't be
embarrassed if she doesn't write back.'

'How can she write back if she doesn't know who
you are?'

'Oh yeah, I never thought of that.' He picked a
scab on his elbow in a thoughtful way. 'Poo bum!
This isn't going to work, is it Brian?'

'Why don't you do what Chris does in *Cyberno*?' I

said. 'Remember how he and Lena stash their secret love letters in the wall of the Space Port?'

'We haven't got a Space Port.'

I added to the end of the letter: *Write your reply and fold it up real small. Then leave it in the crack in the bottom right corner of the climbing wall in the gym.*

'Hey, you're brilliant, Brian!' said Sean.

'No problem,' I said modestly, ripping off the page and tucking it into his shirt pocket. 'Sneak it into her bag before Science and wait to see what happens.'

'Thanks, Brian. I owe you!'

'I won't forget,' I said.

Kids were drifting into the Science lab, dropping their bags outside the room. Sean loitered behind while I went inside, then came in with the last stragglers, giving me a thumbs up. The trap was baited.

It was so easy. Too easy. My nose was itching worse than ever.

At lunchtime, Sean came racing up to Vince and me, triumphantly waving a scrap of paper. 'We're in, Brian! Look what I found in the climbing wall!'

I flattened it out and read:

> Your poem surprised me, I have to admit
> It intrigued me. I'm curious too
> So please won't you tell me, or hint just a bit
> I'm anxious to know — WHO ARE YOU?
> P.S. Email me tonight at honeybabe@supernet.com

'She calls herself "Honeybabe"!' said Vince.

'How hot is that?' gushed Sean. 'But hey, can you email back to her for me, Brian?'

'Me?'

'I don't want her to know who I am just yet. If you stay mysterious and aloof, girls want you even more.'

'Treat 'em mean and keep 'em keen,' said Vince.

'Go on, Brian,' said Sean. 'She'll expect me to write her a real super-hot poem this time.'

I knew I should say no. Writing love letters for someone else was sort of dishonest, even worse than writing excuse notes. But I was desperately curious to see what would happen. Could I really get Jody Helmson to fall in love with Sean Peters, just by writing love letters? If I could do that, I might even make Cassie Wyman fall for someone like me … no, I didn't dare think about that.

Anyway, what was really wrong with what I was doing? When Cyberno writes love letters to help his mate Chris in the play, everybody thinks he's really noble and unselfish. Helping Sean out would be a kind, generous act. I wouldn't be writing any lies. I'd be honestly putting into words the way Sean felt about Jody.

'Okay, I'll do it,' I said.

Sean gave me his email address (<u>hotstuff@supernet.com</u>) and his password, 'cooldude'. Say what you liked about Sean Peters, he certainly believed in thinking positive!

fight choreography n. *fyt kor-io-gra-fee.* Where you make it look like you're really hurting someone or killing them when really it's been worked out like steps in a dance.

THAT afternoon, Joe the stuntman came to DAGS. Elly Gerballo's friend was going to help us stage the battle scenes where Captain Loopy's crew has to fight the aliens with laser lances.

Joe was the coolest guy I ever met in my life. Elly introduced him and told us he was an actor who'd been in films like *Street Fight* and *The Swordsman*. He'd filled in for the stars as a stunt double, because he was a professional at stage fighting, and the real actors couldn't fight for nuts.

Joe took us outside on to the grass by the gym. He worked with us in pairs as we did the sort of mock fights they use in films. He showed us how to throw a stage punch by hitting an imaginary head on our opponent's shoulder. If the person you were hitting jerked their chin towards the blow and clapped their hands at the same time, it really looked like they were being whacked. I was paired with Vince of course, but when it came to demonstrating how to do it, Joe chose Rocco Ferris and Kelvin Moray. They really got into it, swinging and grunting and throwing themselves to the ground as they took punches. I had to admit they were really convincing.

'Hey, we'll have to find you guys a little solo moment in the fight scenes,' promised Joe. Kelvin looked really pleased with himself.

Next we learned how to drag someone around by

How to fight Aliens

{ A GUIDE to using a LASER LANCE by B.Hobble }

No ④ "The Undie Undoer"

the hair. You don't really grab their hair. You just clench your fists and press them on the top of your partner's head. Then your partner holds your wrists and writhes around like they're in agony. Joe demonstrated on Nathan Lumsdyke, and even Nathan managed to look like he was being dragged around.

Then Elly and Lancelot Cummins led the rest of the cast back into the Drama room to rehearse the scenes with the aliens interrogating Captain Loopy, while Joe took Vince and me back into the gym to practise the duel scene, where Cyberno makes up the poem about biffing the alien's bottom.

Joe gave Vince and me each a broomstick to be our laser lances, and showed us how to thrust, lunge, slash and parry. The idea was to make the fight look really dangerous without anyone actually getting hurt. After a few practice moves we were ready to try the scene.

Vince and I took an 'on-guard' position and circled each other, and I said my Cyberno lines:

'You call me rude names, you disgusting green blob,

You're a planetary poo, you're a slimy space slob!'

Vince lunged, I parried, spun him around and kicked him on the bum, calling:

'My laser lance skills, I've just naturally got 'em

So I'll give you a biff on your alien bottom!'

My kick missed, the way it was supposed to, but

Joe showed Vince how to roll with the movement to make it look like he'd taken a huge whack.

Then Vince sprang back to his feet and charged again, slashing with his broom handle. I caught the blow on my stick, held in two hands above my head.

As we struggled, I called:

'Your insults don't hurt me, your words do not cut,

I'll give you a poke in your alien butt!'

I spun around and jammed my stick towards Vince's behind. Again I didn't connect, but from the way Vince screamed and dived into a roll, you'd think he'd been hit by an electric cattle prod charged with a squintillion volts.

'Fantastic!' called Joe. 'Way to go, guys! Finish the scene now.'

I yelled my last lines for the scene:

'You say I look weird? You think that I mind?

I'll give you a belt on your big fat behind!!!'

And as I advanced with my broom handle ready for the death blow, Vince threw himself to the ground and surrendered.

Joe clapped. 'That's it, guys!'

Vince went off to find out if Elly was ready to see what we'd rehearsed. Joe and I were left in the gym.

'Cool climbing wall,' said Joe. 'You get to use it much?'

'We've only done it once,' I said. 'It's only just been re-opened after they got rid of the spiders.'

Vince came back. 'Elly says they need another

twenty minutes to rehearse their scenes, then they'll have a look at our duel.'

'Which gives us time to play on the wall!' said Joe.

Oh no! The last thing I wanted was to let this cool guy see what a wuss I was about heights. 'We're not allowed on the wall,' I said quickly. 'Mr Quale says it's strictly forbidden without a qualified teacher.'

'I'm qualified,' said Joe, flicking a card out of his wallet. 'Gold instructor's certificate from the National Climbing Association.'

'The safety harnesses are in Mr Quale's office,' I said. 'It's locked.'

Joe grinned. 'Hang here a minute, guys.' He whipped out the door and was back two minutes

Climbing gone wrong

A GUIDE by B. Hobble

It's this way!

No. It's this way

LESSON #5:
Don't drop the map!

later laden with ropes, harnesses and carabiners. 'Be prepared,' he said. 'Don't leave home without climbing gear in your car. Right, who's going first?'

'Brian is,' said Vince quickly.

It was bad enough embarrassing myself in front of kids in my class. Now just as I was getting to like Joe, I was going to make an idiot of myself in front of him too. The Wall of Death still scared me stupid.

We strapped on our harnesses and I took up the belaying position.

Joe climbed. The muscles rippled on his shoulders as his arms moved smoothly from grip to grip, his feet switching on a foothold at one point, then powering him to the top. 'Coming down!' he called, letting himself drop onto the harness. The rope jerked tight against the floor anchor, but I was surprised to find that I could take his weight quite easily as I lowered him down.

'Cool route!' he said. 'Your turn, Brian.'

I didn't dare freeze in front of Joe. I took a firm grip on the first two holds and started to climb. My foot slipped off immediately and I slapped down into the floor.

'Hey, wait a minute,' called Joe. 'It's not easy in loose sneakers. I've got some climbing shoes that might fit you.'

With my feet squeezed into the tight rubber shoes, and Joe belaying me, I felt more confident than the first time I'd tried it, and he kept me going by calling encouragement. 'Drive with those legs, Brian … that's the way. Arms are just for balance here. Hang with straight arms, not bent ones – it uses less energy … Well done … switch those feet now …'

The climbing shoes gave me amazing grip on the holds. Before I knew it I was past the spot where I'd got stuck before. I tried the undercling grip I'd seen Joe use to get myself up past hold 12. I was nearly at the top! I glanced down. Joe and Vince were about a million kilometres below me, Joe paying out rope. I was too high up to back down now. I kicked off with my left leg. I flung my arm up to hold 15. I slapped the wall … just short of the hold. I tried desperately to get my balance back, but my body swung away from the wall, ripping my other hand loose.

When the Zoggian pirates make Captain Loopy walk the plank in *Escape from Planet Zog*, he plummets 10,000 metres down to the horrible yellow Pool of Pus. His voice comes as a fading scream of 'Noooooooooooo …!'

As I plummeted off that massive wall, I started to scream too. I won't tell you what the word was, but it was far worse than 'Noooooooooooo …!' Luckily I never needed to finish the rude word, because after I'd fallen six centimetres I was bouncing comfortably in the harness. 'I got you, Brian,' called Joe, taking up the slack. 'Don't worry about the slip, just try that last bit again.'

It was incredible! Now I knew I could trust my safety harness, it didn't feel like I was high at all. I grabbed the handholds again and tried another spring up to hold 15. I caught it this time, and my hand stuck there. Two more heaves with my legs and I was slapping the top like Joe had done, and being lowered to the ground.

Vince and Joe gave me high fives as I touched down.

'See Brian,' said Joe. 'Vertical chess, that's what climbing's like. Using your brains as well as your muscles. If you find the right route, and conserve your energy, you can climb anything. Put the wrong hand in the wrong place and muscles like Mr World's won't get you up there.'

After Vince and I had a few tries, we could do the climb every time. Joe showed us technical tricks like turning our hands over to use undercling grips, and taking the weight on the insides of our feet rather than the toes.

'You guys are doing great,' said Joe. 'This is a cool wall, too. We should do some more next week. Keep the climbing shoes till then.'

By the time Nathan Lumsdyke came in to tell us that actually Elly was actually ready to see the fight scene we'd rehearsed, I was looking forward to Mr Quale's Human Fly comp. I couldn't wait to try climbing again with the rest of the class watching. Next time I'd be able to show them a few new tricks!

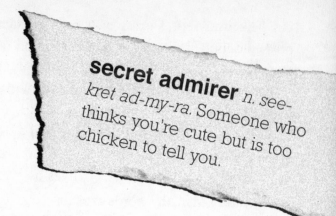

secret admirer *n.* see-kret ad-my-ra. Someone who thinks you're cute but is too chicken to tell you.

NOW I was confident my climbing muscles were in working order, it was time to give my brain muscles a workout too. That night I switched on the computer in Mum's office, logged on and emailed Honeybabe:

> Dear Honeybabe,
> I am a man of mystery
> And yet I like you, as you see
> Your hair, your lips, your nose, your eyes
> They promise me a big surprise.
> And I can sure surprise you too
> Oh Honeybabe, I do like you!
> Mystery Man

I checked it ten times. For some weird reason I was as nervous as if I was sending a real love poem to a girl I liked myself. *This is ridiculous!* I thought, and pressed Send. Then I rang Sean Peters and read the poem out to him.

'Hey, that's cool! Thanks, Brian. That will get her for sure.'

By the time I got back on line, there was Jody Helmson's answer ...

O Mystery Man, thy words are fair
I wonder what you look like there
As I in my imagination
Receive thy anonymous admiration
Please put me out of my misery
Remain not Man of Mystery.
Who are you really?
Honeybabe

Honeybabe was getting a bit flowery, especially the bit about 'thy anonymous admiration', so I thought it would be a good idea to write a flowery poem back again.

My first attempt was terrible:

Dear Honeybabe,
When I look up at thy bottom on the
climbing wall
My heart skips beats, I hopeth that
thee won't fall ...

I pressed Delete. I was sure I could do better than that!

When we did poetry in English, Mr Mackington reckoned the most romantic poet in the entire history of the world was William Shakespeare. Mum had a thick book of his above her desk. There were plays I'd heard of like *Hamlet* and *Macbeth*, and at the back there were all these poems. They were hard to understand, full of 'thees' and 'thous', but they sure looked like love poems.

I could copy one of Shakespeare's sonnets, and maybe Jody would be really impressed if she thought Sean had made it up.

> **Shall I compare thee to a summer's day?**
> **Thou art more lovely and more temperate**
> **Rough winds do shake the darling buds of May**
> **And summer's lease hath all too short a date.**

No way! If I sent her that, Jody would think Sean was a complete loony. Mr Mackington reckons that to write a good love poem, you think about something you like very much and then compare the person you love to that.

So to write a poem that Jody Helmson could understand, I'd have to put something like …

> **Shall I compare thee to a climbing wall?**

No, not good.

> Shall I compare thee to a carabiner?
> I'm hooked on you so don't be meaner

No, that wasn't it either.

> Shall I compare thee to a cool school bubbler
> after a soccer match on a real hot day?
> Shall I compare thee to that gorgeous super-
> hero Mitzi in *Zombie Squad* on TV?

None of them seemed any good at all. I was stuck. I obviously had no talent for writing love poems, and I should just stick to my core business of excuse note forging.

I tried to think what Sean would like about Jody Helmson. My brain went blank. I had no idea. I tried to think what *I* would say to some girl *I* really liked. Cassie Wyman, for instance. She was always surprising me. Just when I thought I'd got to know her, I'd discover something new about her that I'd never suspected. She was like … like something else I really liked.

I had a brilliant idea.

> Shall I compare thee to a Macho Burger?

Suddenly, just as it sometimes happened to Graham in *Think Twice*, my super brain went into hyper-drive. Everything fell into place. I wrote the most fantastic love poem I'd ever written in my life!

> Shall I compare thee to a Macho Burger?
> On the outside, you looketh fairly like a fluffy
> Macho bun,
> All kind of soft and sweet,
> Thy smell, also like a Macho Burger's, is warm
> and inviting,
> It makes me want to nibble you.
> Then biting in, under the crisp lettuce
> There's meat and gristle, and juicy toughness
> you don't expect.
> Oh joy! Thou art not so soft as you seemeth
> And you know how when you finish a Macho
> Burger, bits get stuck between thy teeth and
> are real hard to get rid of? Like, you're a bit
> like that. I sort of can't get thee out of my head.
> Love, Thy Secret Admirer
> (Mythtery Man)

It was the best one I'd done so far. If that didn't get Jody totally begging Sean to go out with her, nothing would.

I checked it and sent it and waited ...

Back came Jody Helmson's answer:

> Dear Secret Admirer,
> I am just soooo impressed! Your poem was

> fantastically funny. It was nice you think I'm
> like a Macho Burger, but I hope you don't think
> I'm so fatty and unhealthy! I try not to be, of
> course. I'm not nearly such a great writer as
> you are, but I'll do my best ...
> Don't be so shy, man of mystery,
> For I can guess who you might be,
> And please believe, I like you too
> And from that liking, you should know
> It's possible that love may grow!
> Honeybabe

Mum came in wearing her dressing gown. 'Brian, it's after ten thirty!' I hit the Minimize sign and Honeybabe rushed down to hide on the bottom panel of the computer screen. 'It's a school day tomorrow. What are you doing?'

'Finishing a poetry assignment,' I said. I held up the Shakespeare book. It was amazing how brilliant I could be under pressure!

'All right,' she said, 'but I'm going to bed. Don't be too late.'

'I won't be, Mum.'

I wrote back to Honeybabe. At first I thought of Sean's interest in Jody's backside when she was climbing ...

> Oh Honeybabe, of all the girls in my class
> Thou has the best suspended arse ...

DELETE!!!! I couldn't send that, not even to embarrass Sean. Instead I thought of Cassie Wyman, and wrote the things I'd always wanted to say to her.

> Oh Honeybabe, of all the kids that goeth to
> school in Garunga,
> It's thee I love, for thee I yearn, for thee my
> heart does hunger
> Hotstuff (the Mystery Man)

And quick as a flash her answer came back and we were chatting on line:

> Oh Mystery Man, now I am sure,
> I know now who thou art,
> Don't be afraid, your lovely words
> have stolen my poor heart.
> Honeybabe

The more messages I wrote, the more the words just started to flow.

> I saw you first as just a friend,
> but now I'll love thee till the end
> (Of time)
> Hotstuff

Two minutes later, there was her reply for me. I mean, for Sean.

I always liked you, but I never
Thought, Hotstuff, that I would ever
Be your very special friend
I love thee too, as I press Send
Honeybabe
P.S. I'm 99% sure I know who you are, Mystery
Man, but just to be certain, please, please put
me out of my misery and tell me.

Jody Helmson was a total utter complete surprise. She'd been in my class for a couple of years, but I never knew she was so good at writing. Or so funny. Or so ... deep breath in, deep breath out ... so romantic. Maybe she was like me – not so great at funny lines when I was talking but good at writing stuff down when there was time to think about it. She was kind of cute too, in a sporty sort of way. Neat little punky haircut, turned up nose. Freckles.

Then I had an evil thought. What would happen if I kept Honeybabe for myself? After all, why shouldn't I? I was doing all the work of winning her, only to hand her over to Sean Peters.

There was another nasty feeling nagging away in the back of my head too. I was being ever so slightly disloyal to Cassie Wyman. For months now she'd been the love of my life, though I'd never told her that. Now just as I was starting to get to know her, another ship was appearing on the horizon of my sea of love, steaming towards me, flags flying gallantly at the top of her beautiful masts … yuck! I can't believe I'm writing muck like that!

I sent Sean Peters a copy of all our correspondence so far, then rang him.

'Did you see what Honeybabe's been writing?' I asked.

'You bet!' he said. 'Fantastic!'

'She says that she likes you,' I said. 'She's even hinting she might love you. Now I have to tell her it's you, Sean.'

'Do you really think so, Brian?'

'Otherwise what's the point of getting her begging to go out with you? You'll find out when you see her tomorrow what she thinks.'

'Okay, Brian. Just do it.'

So I typed back:

Should I tell you?
I am torn
Okay, I will.
My name is Sean (Peters)
(You know, that tall guy.
The one who talks a lot.)

I waited. There was no reply. I waited some more. Nothing. Honeybabe was no longer on line.

117

shocked *n. shokt.* Totally surprised in a nasty way, like you've stuck a screwdriver in a power socket. (Don't try this at home, just because you read it in a book.)

NEXT morning we had P.E. in first period. Jody Helmson didn't disappoint me when I saw her again in person. She looked particularly hot in her climbing gear and the tight harness brought out the best in her bum, even when it wasn't suspended above us. I was a bit jealous of Sean Peters, getting such a cute girlfriend. If he really did get her. In a few minutes I'd know if my love poems had really worked, and 'Honeybabe' Helmson was in love with 'Hotstuff' Peters.

I kept my eyes glued to Jody as Sean came out of the change room. I was like one of those Zoggian guard dogs with staring eyes which can go for three years without blinking. Not once did Jody look in Sean's direction as we lined up in front of the wall. Honeybabe was playing it cool, not making things too easy for Hotstuff.

At first I thought that Sean was playing it cool too.

He didn't look at Jody either. Instead he winked at me, tapped the side of his nose, and started a long conversation with Cassie Wyman. He told her all about an idea he had for the scene in *Cyberno* where Chris tries to talk to Lena Galaxa without Cyberno's help. He demonstrated what he thought Chris should sound like when he gets so nervous his voice goes squeaky.

Then I realised what was really going on. *Seven Eleven's not playing it cool at all,* I thought, *he's completely wussing out! After all my brilliant work getting Honeybabe begging him to be her boyfriend, he doesn't dare go near her.*

Sean's motor mouth kept talking to Cassie until Mr Quale gave him a laser lance look and cleared his throat. 'Attention please, daredevils!' said Mr Quale. 'You'll no doubt be delighted to hear that Brian's spider has been exterminated, and the wall is now ready for the Human Flies. For those of you who think the blue holds we did last time are too easy, try the red holds. Go on, Jody Helmson, show us how it's done.'

The red route had smaller, trickier holds, further apart than the ones on the blue route. Jody rubbed the white chalk on her hands, then climbed steadily, her neat little arms straight and relaxed. She reversed her left hand to undercling hold 13, rocked back and launched herself into a flying 'dymo'. Her hand slapped hold 15, but couldn't grip it, and she fell back to dangle in the harness.

I tore my eyes away from her suspended rear end and glanced sideways. Sean didn't even have the courage to watch her. He was showing Cassie how he thought Chris should gurgle when he can't think of anything to say to Lena.

'Great effort, Jody!' called Mr Quale. 'I don't think anyone's going to get near that today. Who's next?' I looked around the class. Nobody was volunteering.

'Brian Hobble?' said Mr Quale, surprised. I was as surprised as he was. I hadn't meant to move, but somehow my hand had magically stuck itself up into the air.

Mr Quale continued: 'Let's hope you don't find any more dangerous wildlife up on that wall, Brian. Blue holds or red holds?'

My brain hissed in my ear, 'Of course you're not going on those easy blue holds. You are Brian

(Sucker Fingers) Hobble!' 'Red holds,' I heard my voice say.

I took a grip on little red holds 3 and 4. They didn't give me much to hang on to, but by using the straight arms Joe had shown me and keeping my weight on the insides of my rubber climbing shoes, I was amazed to find my nose soon pressing against hold 11, well past the middle of the wall. I swayed back and looked up. I could reach hold 13, but I couldn't get a grip on it. Until I remembered what Jody had done. I turned my hand over to take an undercling grip. I was ready for the leap to hold 15. I rocked back once, twice, then I had a better idea. Hold 14 was tiny, but taking it between my thumb and the side of my finger, the way I'd learned from Joe the stuntman, I could hang on just long enough to move my leg up below me, crank up to hold 15 and ... oops!

I dangled in the harness as Vince belayed me. There was a round of applause from the floor. 'Good effort,' called Mr Quale. 'Brian's the big improver today! The kid is showing more guts than a busy abbatoir.'

I hadn't exactly beaten Jody, but I'd matched her. As Vince lowered me down, I was glowing with pride in my achievement. Was there nothing I couldn't do brilliantly? I'd been so into solving the problems on the climbing wall that I'd forgotten to be scared of heights.

As my feet touched down, the first to pat me on the back was Jody Helmson, eyes shining. 'You were really cranking it, Brian. Using that pinch grip instead of the dymo nearly gave you enough purchase to grab the sloper.' The girl was amazing! She could talk Shakespeare, and she could talk climbing language too. 'You didn't flash the whole route, but you'll get it next time,' she added. 'When you're hot, you're hot.'

'Thanks, Honeybabe,' I said. Jody looked at me sharply. Had I given away too much? I thought.

Sean was still talking to Cassie. It would serve him right if I moved in on Jody. I wondered how she'd react if I came straight out and told her it was me who'd written those brilliant poems. She'd be so surprised to hear that I wasn't just Brian Hobble super climber, but I was also the romantic writing genius? That wouldn't be fair to Sean of course. Or to Cassie.

Although why shouldn't I have more than one girlfriend, if my brain was clever enough to attract them? Evil geniuses were allowed to have as many girlfriends as they liked. In that book *Nose Job*, Professor Mucus had a whole house full of beautiful girls draping themselves around him and passing him tissues when he needed to blow his nose. I'd done all the hard work of winning Honeybabe. I deserved her!

Abby Post was ready to climb, so Jody moved over to belay her. Other kids came and went on the wall. Nobody did quite as well as Jody or I had done, although Vince Peretti nearly reached hold 14. Even Sean Peters seemed a bit distracted and only made it up to hold 10 before slipping off. Maybe his confidence had been dented by finding he didn't have the guts to talk to Honeybabe after all.

I wouldn't say anything to Jody right now. I'd wait till tonight to tell her it was me writing the poems. I could email her again, and this time send a really hot poem. If it worked on Jody, then I could surely get other girls begging to go with me. With email I could contact whoever I liked. I could have a whole harem. I'd be Brian (Hotstuff) Hobble. And after that, when Cassie Wyman came up to me, tears in her eyes, begging to become one of my girlfriends, I would say to her … um …

As we were leaving the gym, Cassie came up to me. There were no tears in her eyes, and she didn't mention wanting to join my harem. Instead, she handed me the book *Cyrano de Bergerac*.

'Nathan thought you might like to be next to read this, Brian,' she said. 'It's a beautiful story, and it's really clever the way Lancelot Cummins has adapted it. He's turned Cyrano into your character Cyberno. Cyrano's in love with a girl called Roxane, who he's made into Lena Galaxa. Cyrano's such a fantastic hero, dashing and gallant and sensitive.'

'Just like me,' I joked.

'And he's so unselfish. Cyrano writes Roxane all these beautiful poems and love letters, but he pretends they came from his friend Christian.'

I knew that. That was exactly what Cyberno does for Chris, and what I'd been doing for Sean Peters. But how did it end? I had to steady my voice as I asked, 'What happens when Roxane finds out it's really Cyrano writing the letters?'

'That's what's so romantic,' said Cassie. 'Roxane never finds out. Even when Christian dies in battle, Cyrano never tells her it was him writing the letters.'

'So Cyrano and Roxane never get together?' I asked.

'At the very end, when they're old, she guesses that all that time it was Cyrano who was in love with her. And all the time she was in love with him.'

'So then Cyrano and Roxane get together?'

'No, then Cyrano dies.'

'Oh.'

'Isn't that just so romantic, Brian?'

'I suppose so.'

It wasn't the ending I would have put in. If I'd been writing it I would have got them together to live happily ever after.

'But if Cyrano really loved Roxane all along,' I said, 'why didn't he just tell her?'

'Because he thought she'd never love him back.'

'Why wouldn't she love him? He's dashing and sensitive and a gallant fighter ...'

'No, you don't understand, Brian. Cyrano's just like your character Cyberno in the play. He knows Roxane won't love him because of his, um, proboscis.'

'His what?'

'You know, Brian, his prominent protuberance. Like in our play everybody admires Cyberno, but he thinks no girl can love him because he's got a ... you know ...'

'A what?'

Cassie laughed and poked her finger at my face. 'You're kidding me, Brian. You really don't know? Cyberno thinks he's ugly because he's got a big nose!'

I was totally flabbergasted, floored and flummoxed! If only I'd looked up those long 'proboscis' and 'protuberance' words when I'd first read them. Brian (Hotstuff) Hobble would never have a harem. He'd never tell Jody he'd written those emails. He'd certainly never dare to tell Cassie Wyman how he felt about her and ask her to be his girlfriend.

Now I knew the awful truth about why Elly had cast me as Cyberno. It wasn't because I was heroic, or dashing, or poetic, or a good writer. She gave me the part in the play because I was the kid in DAGS who had the biggest nose!

Why it's b**a**d to have a BIG NOSE 1

{It makes it hard to drink}

proboscis *n. pro-boss-kiss.* Something huge that sticks out the front of your face so much it would poke out the eye of anyone you tried to kiss. (See also **conk, honker, hooter, snout, nozzle**, etc.)

IT'S hard to get a good look at your own nose. You can try going cross-eyed and staring down, but you get a headache in about .0003 of a second. When you stand in front of a mirror, you only see your nose front on. If you really want to see what your nose looks like from the side, you have to turn your head away and stretch your eyes back towards the mirror. Then you get that headache again. So it's almost impossible to see your nose the way other people see it.

To examine my nose properly, I had to use the laws of physics. I took two mirrors, the bathroom one and the hand mirror Mum uses when she's plucking her eyebrows. I held up the little mirror, and adjusted the angle of incidence and the angle of reflection the way Ms Frankton had shown us in science. It was then that I made a totally terrifying discovery. My nose was not the neat, elegant, manly little thing I'd always imagined it to be. My nose was

humungous! When I looked at it from the side, I saw that my nose was gigantic, colossal, enormous, immense, mountainous and Brobdingnagian (my thesaurus has lots of great words for it, but none of them big enough to describe what I saw). Somehow my nose must have been growing larger and longer, and apart from it feeling itchy from time to time, I'd never noticed.

My little brother Matthew was the first to mention it out loud. At the breakfast table he leaned forward on his chair, his head nearly dangling into his bowl of Crispy Pops, and stared up into my face. 'Brian's got a really big nose, hasn't he, Mummy?' he squeaked.

'Oh, I don't think it's all *that* big,' smiled Mum. She took me by the chin and twisted my head around so she could examine my nose properly. 'Brian's nose is more or less within the normal size range for a boy of his age.'

'But it's growing longer,' Matthew continued tactlessly, 'like in that story about the puppet called Pistachio.'

'You mean Pinocchio,' said Mum. 'And Brian's nose isn't nearly as big as Pinocchio's. Anyway, *Pinocchio*'s just a story to scare naughty children who tell lies.'

'Brian told a lie,' squeaked Matthew. How did he know? I'd never told him about the excuse notes, or the spider on the climbing wall, or my love poems for Sean Peters. 'Brian said he didn't eat the last Choco Fudge Bar in the fridge,' said Matthew, 'but he did, so now his nose is growing longer.'

'Don't be so ridiculous, Matthew,' said Mum. 'Did you eat that Choco Fudge Bar, Brian?'

People say that when you have a major problem it's best to talk about it. But there was nobody I could talk to about my nose growing. My parents would just tell me it was nothing to worry about. Parents are meant to love you however hideously ugly you look.

I thought about going to a doctor, if I could find one who wouldn't tell my parents. Ms Kitto helped me find a medical encyclopaedia in the library. (I told her I was doing a project on chickenpox vaccination.) I looked up what it said about nose-shortening surgery. I found out what doctors call nose-job operations: *rhinoplasty*. How cruel is that? 'Sorry mate, your nose is as big and ugly as a rhino's horn, so I'll cut it off and give you a plastic one instead.' Doctors obviously have no idea how to talk to people who might be sensitive about their nose size.

If you're worried about something so weird and personal, you'd have to be totally crazy to talk to any of your friends about it. I was totally crazy.

'Do I look different to you, Vince?'

'What do you mean "different", Brian?'

'I mean, is my nose … um … bigger?'

'Ginormous, Brian.'

'No, I'm serious, Vince.'

'I'm serious too, Brian. You're famous in Garunga for your humungous honker.'

'Really?'

'Behind your back, Brian, everyone calls you "the Elephant Man".'

'You're kidding, aren't you?'

'We're taking bets on whether you'll grow tusks beside that trunk of yours.'

'Are you serious, Vince?'

'I'm always serious, Brian.'

This wasn't getting me anywhere. When you always talk to your friends in jokes, you don't know when they're telling the truth. So there was nothing I could do about it. Except feel my nose every seventeen seconds to see if it was still growing longer.

Was it just my imagination, or were people talking about noses all the time I was around?

In Science, we were studying natural adaption, examining photos of birds' beaks. Ms Frankton explained that parrots had hard bills for cracking seeds, while ducks had flat beaks for scooping food out of muddy river bottoms. Why did she say, 'Brian Hobble, I'm sure you're just bursting to tell us why honeyeaters have long pointed beaks'? She didn't say, '... long pointed beaks like your nose', but I knew she meant it.

Everywhere I went in the playground, everyone was discussing noses. Abby and Sofie and Sarah were giggling over photos in a fan mag: 'Of *course* he's had a nose job'; 'Everyone *knows* you think he's cute'; 'Shut up, Sarah, you're just being *nosey* ...'

I tried to keep my nose covered with my hand, but I couldn't keep pretending I had something in my eye or an itchy forehead. Besides, at the rate my nose was growing my normal hand wouldn't be big enough to hide it soon. I'd have to start wearing a baseball mitt to conceal my enormous conk.

This was totally freaky. Could it really be that my nose was growing because of the lies I'd been telling? Would it get smaller again if I became more honest?

And what could I do about DAGS? I know not all

actors have to be good-looking. Some actors in films even have big noses, although the big nose actors usually play stuck-up waiters and evil warlords. You never see actors with big noses doing kissing scenes. The directors know the problems that would cause if their noses poked out a girl's eye.

Yet, I was an actor, playing Cyberno, a part where everyone was supposed to laugh at my physical deformity.

That afternoon, Lancelot Cummins brought in a whole lot of new scenes, and it was finally crystal clear what the play was all about. The more we read, the more embarrassed I became. The new scenes were full of nose jokes, with all the space fighters laughing at Cyberno's hooter.

CYBERNO SNEEZES, THEN BLOWS HIS
ENORMOUS NOSE. THE SOUND ECHOES AROUND
THE SPACE PORT. SPACE CADETS COME
RUNNING FROM ALL DIRECTIONS.

SPACE CADET CHRIS: Where's the fire? I
    heard the siren.
CADET 2: Shh! That's not a siren, it's
    just Cyberno blowing his nose.
SPACE CADET CHRIS: Galloping galaxies,
    look at that enormous honker –
    you could park a Space Freighter
    up his nostril!

```
CYBERNO DRAWS HIS LASER LANCE.
EVERYONE SHRINKS BACK. THEY ARE SCARED
OF CYBERNO'S TEMPER AND EXPECT HIM TO
SLAUGHTER SPACE CADET CHRIS.
```

Then I made this really long speech. In verse. All about noses. As I read it, all the DAGS playing space fighters howled with laughter.

```
CYBERNO: You think you can hurt me by
         mocking my nose?
         I've heard it before,
         I know just how it goes.
         Any jest you can make,
         I know what it's about
         'Cause there've been a few jokes
         at the expense of my snout.
         For instance:
         'Cyberno's got a cold - quick,
         get a mop and bucket!'

ALL LAUGH.

         'Cyberno never uses a hanky - he
         wipes his nose with a beach
         towel!'

ALL LAUGH AGAIN.
```

The play was supposed to be a comedy, but this was tragic. When everyone saw me acting this part with this huge nose of mine, I'd never live it down. Brian Hobble nose jokes would make the rest of my life a misery.

I'd have to get out of this play. After the rehearsal, I'd go and talk to Elly and tell her straight that I didn't want to be in it any more. What was the point? I was playing an ugly freak, I wouldn't get to kiss Cassie Wyman, and in the end, my character was going to die.

Of course, Elly would ask why I was leaving the show. I wouldn't be able to say that it was because of my nose. I'd have to think up an excuse, but then I was a world champion in the excuse department. I could pretend to get a throat virus, and lose my voice, and then if I didn't recover the power of speech until after the play was over ...

'Could we read Scene 18 please,' said Elly. 'Brian and Kelvin, isn't it?'

This was another new scene, in which Cyberno wanders out onto the bridge of the spaceship with his true friend Andrew the Android. Kelvin Moray was playing this part, and I had to admit he'd been quite good in the rehearsals so far, especially in the battle scenes, where he walked around hitting aliens with stiff arms. You could easily believe he wasn't quite a human being.

Kelvin said, 'What is the matter with you, Cyberno?'

It took a moment before I realised he was reading Andrew the Android's line from the script. We continued the scene:

ANDREW: What-is-the-matter-with-you-Cyberno?

CYBERNO: It's nothing, Andrew, just a slight pain.

ANDREW: A-pain-where?

CYBERNO: In my ... heart.

ANDREW: I-have-heard-that-you-humans-call-heart-pain-'love'.

CYBERNO: I am in love, Andrew, with Lena Galaxa.

ANDREW: And-does-she-have-heart-pain-too?

CYBERNO: She does, Andrew, but alas not for me. I dare not tell her that I love her.

ANDREW: Cyberno-is-a-brave-fighter-He-should-dare-to-do-anything.

CYBERNO: Not this, Andrew. It's true

Elly interrupted: 'Just hold it there, thanks guys. Brian, you're just reading those lines, as if they don't mean anything.'

'Sorry, Elly?'

'How does Cyberno feel about Lena?' asked Elly.

'He really loves her,' I said.

'And how does he feel about her not loving him?'

'Sad?'

'It's utterly ruining Cyberno's whole life!' said Elly. 'And the only one he can tell is an android, because he's not human, and won't judge him for it.

Try this, Brian: think about something that has gone wrong for you in real life, and keep thinking about it while you read through the scene … Okay, give him the cue again, Kelvin.'

Kelvin repeated the line, only this time he did something I hadn't expected. He stretched out a stiff robot arm and laid it on my shoulder.

ANDREW: Cyberno-is-a-brave-fighter-He-
should-dare-to-do-anything.

CYBERNO: Not this, Andrew. It's true
that I love Lena, but I can never
expect her to love someone as
ugly as me. Not with this huge
ugly protuberance in the middle
of my face. No, it's better that
I set her free, and if my words
can help her to find love with
another man, and be happy, then
perhaps I can find a little
happiness too ...

As I read the speech, I realised I wasn't talking about Lena Galaxa at all. I wasn't playing Cyberno any more, either. I was being Brian Hobble, for once daring to tell someone about his love for Cassie Wyman. I knew she would always be nice to me, because that's the sort of person she was, and she'd always feel sorry for me because of my revolting long nose. But she would never love me the way I loved her.

Then to my horror, I started to cry. All the feelings that I had for Cassie, my disappointment and my guilt came bubbling up inside and squirting out through my eyelids.

When I finished the speech, and looked up, Kelvin was blinking, which is not something you expect an android to do. So was Elly. Cassie Wyman was dabbing the corner of her eye with a handkerchief.

'Kelvin, well done!' said Elly. 'You're the world's first sensitive new age android! And Brian, I just want to tell you how fantastic that performance was. You just *are* Cyberno now. You have a great future if you want to take up acting as a profession some time.'

'Thanks,' I said.

Oh sure, I had a great acting future. Any time there's a part in a play for some blubberer with a huge nose, cast Brian Hobble.

crossroads *n. kros-ro-dz.* Where you can't make up your mind which direction to take because each road leads to something horrible, appalling and totally embarrassing.

REHEARSALS finished for the day, and I walked home alone. I needed time to decide what to do next. Like Captain Loopy when the Zoggians forced him through the Maze of Mystery, I stood at the crossroads, not knowing which path to take. They all looked equally dangerous. But only one road led to the spaceship, Lena Galaxa and freedom. All other roads led straight back to the Great Bog of Zog, a bottomless pit of stinking brown slime from which I would never escape.

The problem was, how could I tell which was the best road to take?

My options were:

(1) I could admit to Elly that I was embarrassed about being cast in the play because of my big nose. I could ask her if someone else could play Cyberno, so I could take on the part of a nor-mal-nosed character.

Problem: She'd say no. She'd say I was great in the play and what was I worried about. She'd say Cyberno was supposed to have a big nose, and I was the only DAG with a hooter big enough to fit the part.

(2) I could tell Mum that I needed emergency plastic surgery to have my nose shortened.

Problem: Mum would tell Dad. Dad would say he couldn't afford it. So Mum would have to pay for it from her own money, and I'd have to go to hospital and have needles, and go into an operation theatre, which would be even scarier than a theatre where they do plays, and people would cut me with knives, and there'd be blood everywhere, and my nose would really hurt, and when I got back to school everyone would say, 'Look at Brian Hobble, he's had *rhinoplasty*.' Then they'd all laugh while they told each other what that word meant.

(3) I could just not turn up to DAGS rehearsals.

Problem: Elly would send someone to ask where I was and that someone would probably be Cassie and then I'd have to tell *her* I was embarrassed about my nose, which would be worse than telling Elly in the first place.

(4) I could stow away on a freighter bound for Argentina, and start a new life, with a new identity, in a far-away country, where nobody

would recognise me.

Problem: Anyone who saw my nose would recognise me straight away, unless I'd had plastic surgery like in point (2) above.

(5) I could stop the whole *Cyberno* show going on, in a clever way so that nobody would suspect it was me that had stopped it. If the play didn't go ahead and I wasn't involved, then DAGS would have to do a different play and I could be in it, but next time not playing the part of someone with a big nose.

Problem: I couldn't think how to stop the show. Unless … unless …

Oh dear, I really was an evil genius! Suddenly my brain kicked in with the most perfect, brilliant, fiendishly wicked idea for stopping the show. It was totally wrong, and selfish, and bad, bad, bad! But it was so simple! All I needed to do was to send one short email, and sign it, 'Concerned Student'.

Which was exactly what I did.

gobsmacked *adj. gob-smakt.* So surprised it's like someone you thought was your friend suddenly pulled a wet fish out of their pocket and smacked you in the gob with it.

AT lunchtime I sat on my own.

Maybe I wasn't an evil genius after all. Evil geniuses aren't supposed to feel bad about their wicked deeds, like I did. After the terrible thing I'd done, I didn't feel like talking to Vince or listening to Sean. They didn't know about my evil deed yet, but in any case they wouldn't want to talk to a freak with a big nose.

Then a voice at my elbow made me jump. 'Brian, can I trust you?' said Cassie Wyman.

'Trust me?' I said. 'Sure you can.' Everybody could trust Brian Hobble. I was a liar, but I was an honest liar.

Cassie cleared her throat. 'Um, I've got this kind of … it's an awkward, um, boy problem.'

'A b-boy problem?'

'I'm not very good at this and I don't know what to do about it. I've never had a boy like me before.'

'Really?' I said. I could feel my face burning and hoped she wouldn't notice.

'Not like me in *that* sort of way, you know. This boy seems to like me, but I don't really like him. Well, I like him, but I don't like, *like* him. Sorry, I'm not making sense. You probably don't have a clue what I mean, Brian.'

'No idea, Cassie.' I was lying again. I had an awful sinking feeling, because I knew exactly what she meant. She was telling me gently she didn't like me. At least not in the way I was hopelessly gone on her. She just called me 'this boy' to spare my feelings.

'I thought I really did like this boy for a while,' said Cassie. 'I liked the way he talks and everything. There's just this problem with ... what he looks like.'

I had to gulp before I asked, 'You mean, you like this boy, except he's ... ugly?'

'I know it's not fair of me, because I think he's a nice person and he's an amazing writer. If you like someone's mind, it isn't supposed to matter what they look like, is it?'

She was talking about me all right. A nice person, an amazing writer, a lovely mind, but just the teensy little problem of having this huge snout sticking out in front of my face.

Cassie was twisting her fingers into a tight knot. 'So what should I tell this boy? I don't want to hurt his feelings. I mean, I don't mind being his friend

143

but I definitely don't want to be his *girlfriend*.'

'And he wants to be your boyfriend?'

'I think he's sort of, you know, in love with me, Brian.'

All the time I thought I'd been hiding it so well and all the time she knew I was crazy about her.

'How do you know "this boy" loves you, Cassie?'

'He sent me emails.'

'Emails?' I said. What was she talking about? I'd never in my life sent Cassie an email. I didn't even know her email address.

'He sent me amazing emails, with the most brilliant love poems. And I emailed him back, because the poems were from someone called "Mystery Man" and I didn't know who he really was. Then I found out it was Sean Peters.'

Sean Peters? I'd kill him! I'd given my so-called friend Seven Eleven all that help, writing poems for him to send to Jody Helmson, and he'd been passing them on to Cassie Wyman as well! Cassie Wyman! My girl friend, who could become my *girlfriend* any time, if it weren't for my nose problem! True, Sean didn't know that I liked Cassie Wyman, but I'd have to kill him anyway.

For all I knew, Sean had emailed my poems to every girl in the entire Universe, just hoping some girl in Greenland or Brazil would write back! He should have told me. The good news was that at least Cassie didn't want to be his boyfriend. She said, 'I just wondered, Brian, if you could sort of, drop Sean a hint?'

'You want me to tell Sean Peters you don't like him?'

'It might sound better coming from you, Brian. I know he's a friend of yours.'

Not any more he's not, I thought. 'Leave it to me,' I said. 'Sean Peters will never bug you again.' When I finished dealing with Seven Eleven there'd be nothing left of him but a pool of green plasma.

'The weird thing is,' said Cassie, 'Sean's emails were so lovely I nearly fell in love with him just from his words. I never realised he was so romantic and funny and ... well, honest.'

Now I started to realise what I might have missed. Did this mean that if Cassie knew the poems were from me, that she would have fallen in love with me too? Maybe I should tell her I'd written the emails. No, I couldn't. Then she'd know I was not just an ugly monster with a big nose, but I was also a *dishonest* ugly big-nosed monster.

I wondered what Cassie had written back to Sean. I'd ask him. He'd tell me. Then I'd kill him.

'How many girls did you send my emails to, Sean?'

'Just Honeybabe, Brian,' said Sean. 'You know that.'

'Then how come Cassie Wyman got them?'

'Because Cassie Wyman *is* Honeybabe.'

'**What????!!!!!!!??????**' I said.

'Who did you think Honeybabe was, Brian? I reckoned Cassie was sort of cute for a while, maybe because Chris is so gone on Lena Galaxa in the play, and I really liked what she wrote back.'

'Hey hold it, Seven Eleven!' I said. The inside of my head was rotating violently like I'd just crawled out of a tail-spinning space rocket. 'Just let me get this clear ... You asked me to write those love poem emails for you ...'

'That's right,' said Sean.

'And you're telling me that all the time "Honeybabe" was *Cassie Wyman*???!!!'

'It's her family's email,' said Sean. 'Cassie reckons her parents call each other "Honey" and "Babe", so as a joke they made that their email name. Didn't you know that?'

I didn't know that. If I had something to say to Cassie I just said it to her. We talked all the time. We were *girl* friend and *boy* friend! I'd never written Cassie an email in my life. Until last week. Blood rushed into my face as I thought about the things I'd written. And what she'd written in reply.

My mind raced back, frantically examining the slow motion replays of my early conversations with Sean. Sean had never actually *said* Jody Helmson was the one he liked. I'd guessed that myself. And I'd guessed wrong. So all the time I thought I'd been writing to Jody, I'd really been writing to Cassie. And she'd been writing back, telling me she was in love! With me! Except she didn't know it was me, and she must have thought . . .

Sean's mouth was open again. 'I've changed my mind about who I like now, Brian, because even though Cassie's kind of cute, I've decided I like Jody Helmson better because she's really hot at climbing, and Jody doesn't like reading too much, so I don't reckon she'd even read email if you sent it to her.'

'I saw you talking to Sean,' said Cassie. 'What did he say?'

'He won't be bothering you any more,' I said. 'He still really likes you, but he's decided he'd rather just be good friends.'

'Oh, phew!' sighed Cassie. 'I was worried he might be really hurt.'

'It's not easy to hurt Sean Peters,' I said. I didn't say anything about him liking Jody Helmson now. I didn't want Cassie's feelings to be hurt either.

'It was funny though,' said Cassie. 'To be honest, I was quite excited about getting those emails. They were really clever and funny and even sort of, well . . . romantic. I thought at first they might have been written by . . .'

Deep breath in, deep breath out. 'Who did you think was writing them, Cassie?'

'At first I thought it was someone who's a really good writer. They had the style of Shakespeare, so it was probably someone who knows about Shakespeare … like Nathan Lumsdyke does.'

'Oh.' So now I knew.

'And then I thought … well, let's just say I was disappointed when I found out it was Sean Peters.'

I was gobsmacked. All this time I'd been thinking I was so awesomely clever. Now I knew for sure I wasn't an evil genius. I was an evil total idiot.

I'd ruined my own life, and I'd done something terrible that was about to ruin things for everybody else too.

Why it's **bad** to have a BIG Nose

Turn right up ahead...

Ay!

{ Giving directions can be dangerous for cyclists }

censorship *n. sen-sor-ship.* Where someone tells you that you can't see something that would be fantastic fun, because it's too rude or scary for someone your age.

'**LADIES** and gentlemen, I'm afraid we have a problem,' said Elly Gerballo.

Lancelot Cummins had just brought in the final scenes of *Cyberno*, and we were supposed to be rehearsing them. Everyone was looking forward to finding out how the story ended. Last week Chris had been killed in a final battle with the Zoggians. Cyberno wrote back to Lena, pretending the letter contained Chris's last words of love for her. Everyone wanted to know if Lena would find out that all along it had been Cyberno writing the letters.

But instead of reading the final scene, Elly called all the DAGS in for a special meeting.

'We have a very serious problem,' she repeated. 'I don't know if any of you have seen this morning's paper ...' She held up a copy of the *Garunga Morning Messenger*. Splashed across the front page was a massive headline that screamed:

49

SCHOOL PLAY HITS ROCKET BOTTOMS!

Kids crowded around to look over Elly's shoulder as she read:

A school play by the popular children's author Lancelot Cummins is causing a stink amongst teachers and parents. A letter from a concerned student from Garunga District School drama group (DAGS) has notified the Morning Messenger *that the play 'contains events and language which may offend'.*

The scence fiction play, Cyberno, *contains numerous references to 'poo, bums and farts', according to our source. In one scene, space fighters power their rocket by pulling down their pants and lighting gas from their own posteriors.*

Author of the well-known Fairy Magic *books Veronica Lovelace, whose son Nathan is a member of DAGS, said: 'I think it is most unfortunate that this sort of smut is considered suitable material for young people. Children's books should contain happy, positive stories, which teach them wholesome values.'*

Lancelot Cummins defended his play's script, saying: 'Thousands of boys and girls seem to enjoy my stories. They are able to make up their own minds about what material they find suitable, and so far as I can see, they are voting with their pocket money and buying my books.'

The director of the play, Ms Elly Gerballo, said that Lancelot Cummins had turned many young people on to reading. 'Ever since we've been rehearsing his play Cyberno, *many students, boys in particular, who would never have considered doing drama, have joined the cast. It would be a great shame if a few narrow-minded elements in the community led to this production not going ahead.'*

The principal of Garunga District School, Mrs Norma Davenport, was not available for comment today.

'Mrs Davenport has asked to read the script,' said Elly, 'and she's told me that if she decides it is offensive, we may need to find another play to do.'

There was a chorus of groans and protests. 'That's not fair, Miss!' 'That's censorship!' 'We'll never find another play as good as *Cyberno*, Miss!'

Elly held up her hands for quiet. 'I've explained to Mrs Davenport that this is still a work in progress, and that I have every confidence in Lancelot Cummins, but as the Garunga principal, she has a responsibility to the parents and the school board. She's promised to make a decision quickly, but we have to face the possibility that we may not be allowed to put *Cyberno* on the stage. So until the matter has been resolved, it's only fair to suspend rehearsals. I'm sorry, I can't say any more. It's up to Mrs Davenport now.'

She slung her bag over her shoulder and walked quickly out of the room. As she passed me, I saw that her lips were pressed tightly together. As soon as she thought she was out of our sight, she rubbed the heel of her hand into her eye. She was trying not to cry.

The DAGS were in shock. It was like the moment in the play when Andrew the Android confesses he's been spying for the Zoggians, after they rewired his circuits.

Then Vince asked the question which was on everybody's lips: 'Who was the "concerned student" who told the paper?'

151

'It's obvious, isn't it?' said Kelvin Moray. 'Whose mother did they quote in the paper? Nathan Lumsdyke always reckons he's too good to read Lancelot Cummins books.'

'Yeah, and Nathan's jealous because Brian Hobble's got the main part,' said Vince.

All eyes in the room turned to point red-hot laser beams at Nathan.

'Actually,' said Nathan. 'Actually, I didn't even know my Mum had read the play ...'

'Oh, yeah?'

'Well, actually ... um ... Mum might just have accidentally found it on my desk ... actually ...'

Blood drained from Nathan Lumsdyke's face as a crowd of DAGS crowded around him. Big angry DAGS, including the toughest thugs in the whole school. It was like the battle scene in the play when the aliens close around the wounded Chris, preparing to turn him into shish kebab with their laser lances.

Even Cassie Wyman was getting in on the act. 'That was a terrible thing to do, Nathan. So many people have worked so hard to get this play on, and now you've let everybody down! I love working on this show and I love being Lena Galaxa and I'll be really disappointed if I can't do it.'

'We done all those rehearsals for nothing!' said Rocco Ferris.

'And what about Elly, Nathan?' said Cassie. 'This

is her first big chance to be a director, and she's doing a fantastic job, and if it doesn't go ahead, will she ever get another job?'

'Maybe not,' muttered Nathan, 'but actually –'

'How's Lancelot Cummins gonna feel when he's writ this whole play and has to cancel it?' said Kelvin. He grabbed Nathan by the collar and pulled back his fist. If he hit him now, it wouldn't be one of those fake stage punches he learned from stunt-man Joe.

'Actually, um . . . ' said Nathan.

Hit the Pause button. Freeze!

If I really had been an evil genius, I would have thought this was all working out perfectly. Nathan would deny writing the letter, but nobody would believe him. The show would be stopped, and Cassie would have to think I was better than Nathan, in spite of my enormous nose.

Nathan Lumsdyke was my Number Two least favourite person in the whole world. Normally I'd be really pleased to see him in this sort of trouble. But my Number One least favourite person in the whole world was me. I'd been a complete total idiot.

In the play, Cyberno arrives just too late to save Chris. He jumps into the circle and heroically fights off the Zoggians, only to find that Chris has already been mortally wounded. I hoped I'd be in time to save Nathan.

Press Play!

'Leave him alone!' I yelled, pushing Kelvin Moray on the chest. 'Get back! Nathan didn't write any letter to the paper.'

'How do you know?' growled Kelvin Moray, releasing Nathan.

This was it. Deep breath in, deep breath out.

'Because *I* wrote it,' I said.

Dead silence fell in the Drama room, like the moment when the laser lance drops from Chris's hand and he dies.

'You, Brian?' asked Vince quietly. 'You were the concerned student?'

'That's right.'

'But why did you do it?' asked Cassie Wyman.

I told them the truth. Not the whole truth, but most of it. I said I was scared about being in the play and I wanted to get out of it, but I was a complete chicken as well as being a complete idiot, so I didn't dare ask Elly to let someone else play Cyberno. I admitted I'd been so busy thinking about myself and my problems, that I hadn't noticed how important the play was to everybody else in the cast.

I didn't tell them I was embarrassed about my nose. That was obvious. My nose was sticking out a mile.

'I wish I hadn't done it now,' I finished lamely. 'Now I really want this play to go on, and I want to play Cyberno. You can bash me up if you like. I deserve it.'

'Nobody's going to bash you, Brian,' said Cassie firmly. She laid a hand on my arm and turned to the others, as if daring them to prove her wrong. 'But what are we going to do about it?'

My brilliant genius brain had slipped out of the Drama room window as soon as it saw me getting into trouble. Instead, my ordinary old brain had an idea. Not a clever idea. Just something everyday and normal and honest, which might put things right.

own up *v. o-nup.* Plead guilty, confess, admit, blurt, blab and blather that the things that have gone horribly wrong are all your fault.

LANCELOT Cummins says the scariest place in the Universe is the Zoggian Inquisition Chamber. He's a fantastic writer, but he doesn't know fear the way I do. The scariest place in the entire Universe is Mrs Davenport's office at Garunga District School when you've done something wrong. I know, because I've been there.

The principal's office is at its scariest when you're there on your own, waiting for Mrs Davenport to arrive. You have time to imagine the terrible things that are going to happen when she comes through that door.

I could hear Mrs Davenport's laser lance voice coming from the corridor outside, slicing up three senior boys who'd been caught out of bounds, playing 'Blood Bath' at Garunga Video Arcade. 'This is *not* the sort of behaviour expected from Garunga students. I am *absolutely outraged* by your *disgraceful* conduct ...' I could imagine the toughest kids in the school melting in front of her like ice creams dropped on a hot footpath.

It would be my turn next. My heart was pounding, my palms were dripping and someone had turned on taps in both my armpits. I sneaked a puff on my asthma inhaler and tried to settle my breathing and shut the bad thoughts out of my mind.

That suddenly became easier to do, because my eye was caught by a pinboard on Mrs Davenport's office wall. It was covered with excuse notes. My excuse notes. Dozens of them.

Sofie's papier mache art project was destroyed when an escaped elephant trampled her schoolbag ...

Please let Mario off detention today.
He has an urgent appointment at the
Astronaut Space Training Centre ...

Nicholas apologises for breaking school rules and bringing his mobile phone to school. He is starring in a movie and needed to contact a famous Hollywood film producer ...

Each excuse was numbered. The spelling and grammar were corrected with red ink. There was a mark out of ten at the bottom of each one.

For a moment I didn't understand why they were there. Then the horrible truth dawned on me. The teachers had only *pretended* to believe the excuse notes while they laid a trap for the writing criminal. They'd been collecting the notes and sending them to Mrs Davenport. She'd probably told the FBI, the CIA and Scotland Yard detectives, and they'd all be trying to catch the great Excuse Note Mastermind.

When they discovered I'd written them, a terrible punishment would surely await me. It would be humiliating and public, probably at a whole school assembly. Like when the inquisitors hung Captain Loopy upside down in his underpants, and then set fire to them.

I heard Mrs Davenport dismiss the Video Arcade Gang. For a moment I thought of making a dash for it. I could climb out the office window. It was two floors to the ground below, but at that moment splattering on concrete seemed better than facing Mrs Davenport. I was too slow. She swept in through the door, booming, 'Well, well, well, Mr Brian Hobble! To what do I owe the pleasure of this visit?'

I tried to keep my voice steady and sensible, but it came out like one of those squeaks Sean Peters did in the play when he was talking to Lena Galaxa. 'Um ... eek ... squitchh ...'

My eye flickered to the pinboard again. Mrs Davenport followed my line of sight, then bored her laser lance gaze into my brain. 'I see you like my little excuse note collection,' she said. 'As a creative writer yourself, you'd appreciate the talent of the students *or student* responsible for dreaming up these fantasies. Wouldn't you, Brian?'

Somehow my tongue had become twisted into a double reef knot. 'Skrttt … ee … um, Miss,' I said.

'What amazes me is that the author of these fabulous myths apparently expected intelligent educators to believe them. Can you imagine any teacher at this school actually accepting excuses like these, Mr Hobble?'

'Um, squikkll … no, Miss.'

Mrs Davenport smiled a terrifying smile. When Zoggian inquisitors do this you know you're in big trouble. 'The last few weeks these excuse notes have become so creative that we've instituted a little staffroom competition. The teacher who collects the most outrageous excuse will win a bottle of fine red wine at the celebratory end-of-term dinner.' So that was the solution to the freaky mystery! There hadn't been any supernatural forces making teachers accept my excuse notes. They'd just been pretending to swallow them, so they could swallow some of Mrs Davenport's wine.

Mrs Davenport continued: 'The editors of the *Garunga School Gazette* are considering publishing the most inventive excuse notes in their Creative Fiction pages. What do you think of that idea, Brian?'

Her gaze bored straight through my head, to where my brilliant brain was trying to hide behind my normal stupid brain, leaving my mouth to do the talking on its own. 'Cheeblttt . . .' said my mouth.

'Such a shame that the imagination shown in thinking up excuses could not be channelled into completing schoolwork. Don't you agree, Mr Hobble?'

My mouth was so scared, it would agree to anything Mrs Davenport suggested. 'Shuch a sh-shame, Miss.'

There was a pause. Mrs Davenport looked at me. I looked at her. She looked at me some more. 'You requested this little meeting, Brian. What did you want to see me about?'

There was no escape now. 'Well, you see, Miss, it's like this, Miss, it's all about the fact of, um, Miss . . . what I was thinking was . . .'

'Yes?'

My mouth had had enough. It spat out the reef knot and blurted, 'Miss-you-know-how-a-con-cerned-student-wrote-to-the-paper-Miss-about-*Cyb erno*-being-unsuitable-for-children-Miss?'

'Yes?'

My voice faltered to a whisper. 'The concerned student . . . was me. Miss.'

Mrs Davenport said nothing. She just raised one eyebrow, evil warlord-style.

I told her everything. About me being scared to go in the play and trying to get it stopped. I told her how I'd changed my mind when I saw how disappointed everyone was. 'So now I want the play to go on,' I said.

Mrs Davenport touched the tips of her fingers together and looked up at the ceiling.

'I do not approve of anonymous letters, Brian. If people have something to say, they should be brave enough to say it publicly and be prepared to stand by their views and argue the case. Signing yourself "Concerned Student" was the act of a coward.'

'Yes, Miss.'

'However, I imagine this trip to tell me about it wasn't easy.'

It sure hadn't been easy. It was the hardest thing I'd ever done in my life.

'It takes courage to be honest when you've done something wrong, and for that I thank you, Brian.'

'Um, that's all right, Miss.'

There was another of those pauses. Mrs Davenport said, 'And . . . ?'

My mouth blurted out, 'And-I-wrote-those-excuse-notes-Miss.'

Mrs Davenport's second eyebrow rose slowly to join her evil warlord one. 'All of them, Brian?'

'I know I shouldn't have done it, Miss, but the

reason I did it was ... was ... there wasn't any reason, Miss. I was sort of showing off. I thought I was being clever.'

Mrs Davenport crossed to the excuses on the pinboard. She didn't exactly walk, she sort of flowed there – like a giant iceberg sailing in an ocean current.

'The traffic jam excuse is not clever.'

'No, Miss.'

'Nor is helping the police foil a jewel robbery.'

'No, Miss.'

'I think my favourite is the circus train with the escaped seals.'

'Miss?'

'Don't do it again, Brian. Or there will be *serious repercussions*!'

'No, Miss. I mean, yes Miss, I mean ...'

'Now, about this *Cyberno* play ...'

'It's got to go on, Miss,' I said. 'It's a really good Lancelot Cummins play, Miss, and everyone's worked really hard on it, and the little kids in the audience won't be shocked, Miss, and even the parents will just think it's really funny ...'

'You mistake me, Brian,' said Mrs Davenport. 'I've read the script. I think it's very clever.'

'Do you, Miss?'

'Brian, I think people should be allowed to make up their own minds about what's suitable for them and their children to see. All the same, we have a problem. The press have the story now and you know how they love a scandal. I've told them that I stand behind the production and that I trust Mr Cummins, Ms Gerballo and the cast to do the school proud. Now I have been invited to appear on the television program *Good Morning Garunga* to argue the case for *Cyberno*, debating its merits with Nathan Lumsdyke's mother, Veronica Lovelace. She feels the play is unsuitable.'

'I know, Miss.'

'I am not looking forward to this debate. It will take place in front of a live studio audience, and will be closely watched by many of this school's parents and board members, not to mention those who would like to see this school in trouble. I have decided not to appear on the program.'

'Miss, won't that mean they'll just have Nathan's mum saying how bad the show is? If nobody's there to argue with her, people will think she's right.'

'Exactly, Brian. But I think it would better to send someone else to argue the case for *Cyberno*. Someone who knows more than I do about the sort of stories young people enjoy.'

'You mean Lancelot Cummins, Miss?'

'No, Brian. I mean you.'

'Me, Mrs Davenport?'

'You have committed a string of crimes and misdemeanours, Brian, and it is only right that you should atone for them.'

'Yes, Miss.'

'I could put you on detention. I could make you write out one thousand times "I must not be an arrogant little fool." I see little point in such punishments. You have provided my staff with some light entertainment, but you have already wasted too much of their valuable time. Furthermore, you have brought this school to the brink of disrepute.'

'Miss?'

'You got the school into this mess, Brian. Your punishment will be to appear on *Good Morning Garunga*, accompanied by some of your fellow cast members. You will publicly take the blame for this shemozzle and set the record straight.'

CASSIE Wyman was even more nervous than I was. Her hands were trembling as she pored over her script and mouthed her lines at double speed.

'You'll be fine, Cassie,' I said. 'All you have to do is forget there's a studio audience.' As well as thousands of viewers watching *Good Morning Garunga* on TV, I thought. Including everyone we know.

Cassie and I were 'relaxing' in the studio Green Room, waiting to be called onto the set. On the monitor in the corner, the hosts, Chad and Suzy, were interviewing a lady who bred hairless cats. In the room next to us, Nathan Lumsdyke was getting his face plastered with make-up.

I'd never been less relaxed in my life. I was totally terrified. The idea was that after we'd discussed the play with Veronica Lovelace and Nathan, Cassie and I would act out a short scene in the TV studio.

We'd chosen the balcony scene in which Cyberno speaks for shy Chris, wooing Lena Galaxa with his love poetry, before Chris climbs up to give Lena a kiss.

CYBERNO: Oh Lena dear,
    your slightest glance
    Cuts through me
    like a laser lance
    I wish I could, I wish I might
    Go round you like a satellite

LENA: You press my buttons,
    You stir my soul,
    You are my one command control
    Your lovely words,
    oh how I'll miss 'em
    As I fly through the Solar System

CYBERNO: Take me to the stars
    With your dazzling smiles
    You spriggle my sprockets
    You twiddle my dials,
    Though I must go to Planet Zog
    To save the Earth
    from being a Bog,
    I'll think of Lena, before I die
    You are my oxygen supply.

We'd just done a quick run-through of the lines in the Green Room, but somehow it didn't seem as funny as it had at school, with all our friends laughing and hooting encouragement.

'On set please,' called the production assistant. 'We're going live after the commercial break.'

She ushered Cassie, Nathan and me in, to sit in an awkward row on a sofa. The hosts Chad and Suzy introduced us. 'Brian, Cassie and Nathan are actors in what may turn out to be the most offensive play in the Galaxy,' grinned cheery Suzy. 'It's *Cyberno*, by Lancelot Cummins, and it's causing quite a stink around Garunga,' said Chad.

Chad turned to the elegant lady lounging in an armchair opposite us. 'Veronica Lovelace, as well as being Nathan's mother, is the author of the popular *Fairy Magic* books. Veronica, what exactly is your objection to this play *Cyberno*?'

Veronica smiled the smile of a particularly vicious Zoggian inquisitor. 'Well, as a writer of over fifty *extremely* popular books, I should think I know what's appropriate for children and what isn't.'

'And you don't think *Cyberno* is appropriate?' asked Chad.

'Absolutely inappropriate!' said Veronica. 'Like too many of Lancelot Cummins' books, it's full of disgusting language and poor attempts at humour about ... bodily functions.'

'Well, let's ask the kids if they find it offensive,' said Suzy. 'Let's start with Brian.'

The camera opposite me moved in closer.

Suddenly the studio had been turned into a Zoggian Fart Oven with the temperature at 2,000,000,000 degrees. A small river of sweat ran down the back of my spine.

'Um,' I mumbled. 'I was the c-concerned s-student who wrote the letter to the p-paper saying the play was no good, but really I w-wasn't off-offended at all ... really I like it.'

'And what do you like about the play, Brian?' asked Chad.

'It's ... er ... funny.'

'You enjoy reading Lancelot Cummins books, do you Brian?' asked Suzy. 'Do you think they're suitable for readers of your age?'

'Um ... yes,' I said. 'His books are the only ones I read.' Oops! I shouldn't have said that. I was coming across as a total complete idiot. Unless I could find something more convincing to say, the play would be cancelled.

Before I could add anything, Veronica Lovelace jumped in. 'We hear a lot about what a great job Lancelot Cummins has done in turning young readers on to books,' she said. 'His work is very popular, and even some librarians tell me, "I don't care what they read, as long as they read something." But I ask you, what is the point of reading at all if it's stuff like this ... ?' She held out her hand, and Nathan passed his mother a script, marked with yellow tags. She found a spot and read:

'You pus-ridden wart, you revolting young blob,
You planetary poop, you snivelling snob . . .'

She turned the page and found another line: 'I'll give you a biff on your alien bottom!'

The studio audience was supposed to be revolted by this, but I noticed that a few of them smiled. Even Chad grinned as Veronica flipped to another page. 'There are thousands of better plays this group could be doing. I mean, listen to this shallow muck . . .' And to my total shock and horror, she read out:

'Take me to the stars
With your dazzling smiles
You spriggle my sprockets
You twiddle my dials,
Though I must go to Planet Zog
To save the Earth from being a bog,
I'll think of Lena, before I die
You are my oxygen supply.'

When I heard it read out in Veronica Lovelace's voice, with rounded vowels and exaggerated sing-songy rhythms, the scene sounded totally ridiculous. It wasn't funny, it wasn't moving, it was . . . nothing. In two minutes Cassie and I would be acting this shallow muck for thousands of people to see.

'Well, I wonder if Brian agrees,' said Chad.

A small alien was hanging on to my tongue, stopping it from working properly. 'It . . . uh, sounds worse when you . . . um, take it out of context,' I fumbled out. 'Lots of books sound bad if you just hear little bits of them, like, er, um ... like ...'

I'd meant to quote something here myself. I'd memorised a few lines out of Veronica Lovelace's books. Her cutesy *Fairy Magic* books were full of stuff much more revolting than any 'planetary poops' or 'alien bottoms'. The bits about fairy tea-parties among the bluebells and pixies riding butterflies would sound ridiculous too.

Unfortunately just as I opened my mouth to recite them, I caught sight of myself in one of the TV monitors. The camera was filming me from side on, and I could see my nose. It was totally gigantic! I was so obsessed by the sight of my appalling snout that the *Fairy Magic* lines were wiped out of my head, leaving me blushing and wishing *Good Morning Garunga* would suddenly be swept away by a small landslide.

Why it's bad to have a BIG NOSE 5 (It can be really hard to keep clean)...

My mouth opened and shut like Madeline Chubb's goldfish, until Cassie came to my rescue. 'Could I say something?' she said.

'Yes, Cassandra?' said Suzy.

'There are lots of kids doing *Cyberno* who've never been in a play before. They may have joined our DAGS group for all sorts of reasons ...' she glanced across at me as she said this, '... but they've stayed because they really like Lancelot Cummins' play. He uses great characters and funny lines, on a level that all kids can relate to, not just intellectual kids, but all sorts of kids.'

'Students like my son Nathan are actually capable of acting in much better plays,' said Veronica. 'Nathan has actually been reading adult books since he was ten. And this rubbish is beneath him.'

'And why is it beneath you, Nathan?' asked Chad.

'Well, actually –' began Nathan, but his mother cut him off, saying, 'Nathan actually thinks that *Cyberno* offers nothing uplifting or educating, or challenging to young minds ...'

'Actually,' said Nathan, 'I think –'

'Nathan!' said Veronica Lovelace.

'Please let me speak for myself, Mum,' said Nathan firmly.

'Yes,' said Suzy, 'we'd like to hear from Nathan.'

'Very well, if that's how you feel,' said Veronica Lovelace.

She then settled back into her chair, adjusting her

sleeves like a hen that's been accidentally squirted with a garden hose.

'Actually,' said Nathan, 'as well as being funny, *Cyberno* actually contains a lot of interesting ideas.'

'What sort of ideas?' asked Suzy.

'It's a play full of fighting, but it's actually against war,' said Nathan. 'And it's a love story, but it actually asks us to think seriously about whether we fall in love with someone's appearance or with what's actually inside them.'

For once I was pleased that Nathan was with us. He'd said something really sensible and impressive. And he'd been very brave to stand up to his mum.

'Very interesting point of view, Nathan,' interrupted Chad. 'But so our audience here and you viewers at home can make up your own minds, we'll let the play speak for itself. These young actors have agreed to do a short scene for us so we can see what *Cyberno*'s all about. Over to you, Brian and Cassandra!'

The studio assistant held up an *Applause* sign and the audience clapped politely. Cassie and I edged across to where two chairs had been set up.

'We can't do the love letter scene,' hissed Cassie out of the corner of her mouth. 'It will sound terrible now that Veronica Lovelace has read it.'

'Let's do the last scene in the play,' I whispered back. 'The one that Lancelot Cummins gave us yesterday.'

'But we haven't rehearsed it,' protested Cassie. 'I've only read it once.'

'And what did you think of it?'

'Brilliant,' she said simply.

The ripple of polite applause had died down. It was dead quiet in the studio as everybody waited for us to start.

'So?' I whispered.

'Okay,' whispered Cassie.

I turned to the camera and quickly explained the story so far. 'When Chris is killed, Lena is grief-stricken. She thinks she's lost the love of her life, but her only comfort is that her friend Cyberno has come back from the war on Planet Zog. Then she realises that Cyberno has been badly wounded in the battle.'

Then we read the scene. It wasn't funny. It wasn't meant to be. It was a desperately sad scene in which Lena realised it was Cyberno she truly loved, and she'd ignored him because of his ugly nose. And now he'd come to see her one last time, because he was dying of his wounds.

```
LENA:  I don't know what to say,
       Cyberno ... I've ruined your
       life.
CYBERNO: You, Lena? Never. My mother
       thought I was unattractive. My
       fellow space fighters thought I
```

> was amusing. But you always
> treated me kindly, Lena. In you,
> I had ... a friend.

As we read the scene, the studio audience watched quietly. Seriously.

> **CYBERNO:** When I wrote those poems for
> Chris to say to you, that summed
> up my life. I was always in the
> background, scribbling my words.
> While others climbed into the
> light of the balcony to receive
> the glory, the cheers ... and the
> kisses.

It was an extraordinary scene. It was about Cyberno and Lena, but it was about lots of other things too. Cyberno could be talking about any writer. This could be Lancelot Cummins himself, a famous playwright who writes the brilliant words, then shrinks shyly away to the back of the theatre while the actors who speak his lines become the stars.

When he talks about his battles, Cyberno says:

> Why do we fight? Why do we
> struggle? Not to win.
> Even when the cause is lost,
> the glory is in fighting on!

He's not just talking about a battle with the Zoggians, he's talking about anyone who fights for a cause because they believe it's the right thing to do. This was a wonderful play, which had so much to say on lots of different levels. No way was it shallow muck.

When I died in Lena's arms at the end of the scene, there was silence in the studio. Then everyone was on their feet, clapping and cheering as Cassie and I took a bow.

'Wow!' said Suzy. 'Chad, this is one play that we shouldn't miss!'

Even Nathan was clapping us. Veronica Lovelace was politely tapping her hands together.

'You know the old saying, Suzy,' said Chad, '"The show must go on"!'

So there was good news and bad news. The good news was that *Cyberno* would go on. The bad news was, I'd have to be in it. And so would my nose.

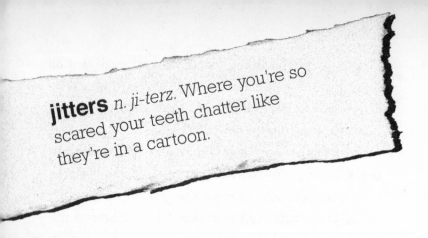

jitters *n. ji-terz.* Where you're so scared your teeth chatter like they're in a cartoon.

THERE'S a terrifying chapter in *Escape from Planet Zog*. Captain Loopy's crew are stuck down a sewer and the revolting brown water starts to rise, forcing them all up against the metal grating. Everybody's panicking, yelling and screaming and blaming each other for what's gone wrong. Andrew the Android gets so nervous he pulls his own head off.

Our dressing room, as we prepared for the first performance of *Cyberno*, was exactly like that. Too many kids, too little space and everything going wrong all at once. Aliens and space fighters fighting and squabbling and accusing each other. Panic was rising like brown sewage and threatening to choke the lot of us. Kids pulled on uncomfortable new costumes and forgot where they'd put their props.

'Who took my rubber alien ears?' yelled Madeline Chubb.

'My space fighter jacket doesn't fit!' wailed Leeanne.

'You got it on back to front, ya dummy,' snapped Vince Peretti.

Kelvin and Rocco were practising moves for their fight, amid protests from kids who got jabbed by their whirring laser lances.

Through the scrum of tangled bodies waded the calm figure of Elly Gerballo, like Lena Galaxa when she unlocks the metal grating, frees the crew and bolts Andrew the Android's head back on.

Elly clapped her hands to get attention. 'There's no need for panic,' she said. 'This is a preview, so treat it as just another rehearsal. The only reason we have an audience at all is because there's been so much interest in the show that we couldn't offer performance tickets to all the people who wanted to see it. People know you're wearing your costumes for the first time, so I've warned them that we may have to stop and fix a scene or two if things go badly wrong.'

If things went badly wrong! What could go wrong that hadn't already gone wrong? I was going to spend the next three nights with people publicly pointing and laughing and making jokes about my huge nose.

Lines I was supposed to say ran around my head in a confused jumble: 'I'm Cyberno, the super poet, I'm a lover and I know it, Clear a path for me, don't blow it ... You think you're tough, you scum of Zog! You're softer than a chocolate frog, Melting in the sun all day ...'

The more I tried to remember them, the more my brain tangled them ... 'I'm Cyberno the chocolate frog, I'm a scummy Zoggy dog ...' I couldn't do this! I'd get out there in the blinding lights and I was sure I'd forget everything I was supposed to say and do. The show would be a total, complete and utter disaster and it would all be my fault!

I buttoned up my space fighter's jacket, and slipped out of the dressing room and along the corridor to the quiet of the toilets. At least, it should have been quiet. The door of one of the cubicles was shut and behind it I could hear a horrible retching sound. Someone was throwing up. I was about to sneak out into the corridor before anyone knew I'd been there, but the toilet flushed, the door opened and out came the great Lancelot Cummins, wiping his mouth with the back of his hand.

I didn't know where to look. 'Um ... hi, Lance,' I said, trying to sound like nothing special had happened.

'Hello, Brian,' he grinned sheepishly. A little colour ran back into his cheeks. 'I suppose you heard that.'

'Heard what?' I said, doing my best to act totally ignorant.

'Nerves,' said Lance, rinsing his mouth at the

washbasin. 'Ridiculous, at my age. It's just a school play, but I'm still scared stiff to see my work go on stage.'

'There's no need to worry, Lance,' I said. 'Everyone's sure *Cyberno*'s going to be great.' I was lying again, but this time for a very good cause.

Lance washed his hands. 'I'm not nervous for myself, or even for the audience. I'm nervous for you actors and Elly and the people who've worked so hard to put this show on. I'm more grateful to you all than I can say, and if it turns out that the script isn't good, I'll feel I've let everybody down.'

'You haven't let us down, Lance,' I said. 'We're really lucky you wrote such a fantastic play for us.'

'Thanks for the encouragement, Brian,' said Lancelot Cummins, 'and good luck to you too. This is your show now.' He gave me a pat on the shoulder and left.

When I got back to the dressing room, the atmosphere had calmed down and the smell of make-up had replaced the smell of fear. I calmed down too. For about thirty seconds.

Then Cassie Wyman came in, and for the first time I saw her in her Lena Galaxa costume. Oh dear, how beautiful she was!

Her blonde hair was tied up in tight buns on either side of her head. In normal life she didn't wear make-up, but now fine black lines were painted around her eyes and her lips were bright red. She looked totally glamorous and completely to die for.

The sight of her started my mouth babbling. I couldn't stop it. 'Your hair, your lips, your nose, your eyes,' I found I was murmuring.

'... They promise me a big surprise,' she answered. Then she blushed bright red.

'You *remember* that email poem?' I said.

'So do you, Brian,' said Cassie. 'Did your friend Sean Peters show it to you?' Her eyes were boring into me, Zoggian inquisitor-style. The temperature in the dressing room was rising fast, and I knew my face was blushing bright red too. It was time for my brain to think up another brilliant lie, but somehow I didn't want it to.

'Sean didn't show me the poem,' I said.

'He didn't need to, did he Brian?'

'No.'

'Or should I maybe call you ... "Hotstuff"?' Cassie the Zoggian inquisitor knew!

So I told her everything. I explained how Sean asked me to help him, and I thought I was sending the emails to Jody Helmson, but as I was making up the poems I was thinking about what I'd like to say to Cassie if I dared. And when Honeybabe had written those love letters back to Hotstuff ...

Just a minute, let me think! Cassie didn't know at first that Sean Peters *was* Hotstuff, so when she wrote back ... Now I had a Zoggian inquisitor question for her!

'Who did you *think* was writing those poems, Cassie? You said you were surprised when you found out it was Sean.'

'At first I wondered if, I mean, I was nearly sure ...' I thought she was already as red as a girl could ever be, but now she blushed even more. 'I *hoped* it was you, Brian.'

'Me?' So when she sent all that stuff about 'from that liking, love may grow', she thought she was writing to me!

'Brian, why didn't you just tell me to my face you felt that way? Girls like to be told if someone likes them.'

'I was embarrassed, the same as Cyberno in the play. I know you don't like the way I look.'

'What's wrong with the way you look?' she asked.

'Well, I've got this sort of larger-than-normal ... oh, please don't make me say it,' I mumbled, pretending to scratch my nose, but doing my best to hide it with my hand. This was torture!

Cassie looked straight into my face again. 'Brian, you're not so bad-looking, you know. I've been too shy to say it before, but I've always thought you were kind of ... cute.' That was typical Cassie Wyman, trying to make social rejects feel good. She was sparing my feelings by not mentioning my hideous, deformed, humungous nose.

'Oh, there you are, Brian,' interrupted Elly Gerballo. 'I was afraid I'd lost you. Try this on for

size.' She handed me a massive rubber nose, with a mole on the end. 'Stick it on with the airholes underneath, so you can still breathe. We can't have Cyberno dying of lack of oxygen in Act One.'

A rubber nose? A huge ugly conk. 'Do I really need to wear it?' I asked.

'Of course, Brian, it's a vital part of your costume,' she said. 'The whole play's about Cyberno's big nose, so it wouldn't make sense if you went out there with just a normal little nose like your real one.'

Did she just say my real nose was normal? And little? 'But I thought . . .' I stammered. 'Isn't my nose . . . ?' I stopped as Elly bustled away. I'd just caught a glimpse of my face in the dressing room mirror. And

I saw something incredible. My nose was short again. Normal!

It was impossible that Cassie hadn't noticed the difference, but she gave no sign that anything strange had happened.

'Did you just say you think I'm cute, Cassie?'

'Especially in that space fighter suit. You're real film star material, Brian.'

I slipped on the rubber nose. 'And now?'

Cassie giggled. 'Still not bad.' Then she said, seriously, 'I can see past a big nose, you know, Brian. And I like what I see behind it. You're pretty hot, Hotstuff!'

I wanted to kiss her, but I was afraid my rubber nose would fall off, or poke her in the eye.

'Hey, check out Cyberno's hooter!' called Vince. Everyone turned to look at me. Everyone was laughing at my rubber nose. Hadn't they noticed how big my real nose had been?

An android pushed roughly past me, jabbing me in the ear with the corner of his cardboard box head. 'Oops, sorry Brian,' said Kelvin Moray. 'Are you okay?'

'Sure, Kelvin,' I said. 'Your costume looks great, by the way.' And it did.

'Thanks Brian,' he said. 'This whole play's a blast, isn't it? Thanks for getting me into it.'

'Any time, Kelvin,' I said. He punched me on the arm.

'Break a leg, Cassie,' came Nathan Lumsdyke's voice behind me.

'Thanks, Nathan,' said Cassie.

I whipped around, in time to see them shaking hands, rather formally. Then Nathan turned to me. 'Actually, Brian, I think you'll be rather good in this play. Good luck.' He held out his hand. I took it and said, 'Good luck to you too, Nathan. You're great as Captain Loopy. See you on stage.'

'Standing by everyone, please,' called Elly. 'Beginners in positions please, and wait for the curtain to rise. And no talking backstage, Sean Peters!'

Vince discovered a crack in the Space Port set, and we all took turns looking out through it as the audience flooded into the hall. Everyone was out there – kids, teachers, Mum, Dad, Matthew, Mrs Davenport. There was even a reporter from the *Garunga Morning Messenger*, and TV news cameras.

'There's no such thing as bad publicity,' whispered Elly Gerballo. 'We've got a full house! Now good luck everyone! Have fun! Cue one – go!'

Music blared as Nathan Lumsdyke and the space fighters marched on stage. As I waited for my entrance, I checked myself out in the mirror set up in the wings for people doing quick costume changes. I adjusted my rubber nose. Cassie Wyman thought I was cute! Film star material. Now I thought of it, maybe I wasn't too bad. Cyberno's space fighter costume suited me. Even my rubber nose wouldn't stop people thinking I was a really handsome super-spunk!

Then suddenly I saw a problem. How come I hadn't noticed it before? My ears. They were huge, enormous ... elephantine! I was about to go on stage with appendages that looked like I'd borrowed them from a Zoggian guard who could hear a whisper at a distance of seven kilometres. My ears were a total embarrassment! I had to get out of this play!

'No problem, Brian!' said my brilliant brain, coming round the corner to rescue me. 'Stage an asthma attack. Just tell someone you're out of breath and you can't go on.' I pulled my puffer from my pocket. Then I put it away again.

I'd had enough of being brilliant. I wanted to be just normal Brian Hobble, nothing-special-looking kid, who was going to walk on stage and do his best.

'How about you fake a major heart attack?' whispered my genius brain. 'Just clutch your chest and fall over backwards ...'

'Shut up, brain,' I said. 'I don't need you any more.' I clamped my space fighter's helmet over my humungous ugly ears. I was Brian Hobble, otherwise known as Cyberno. I was a poet, a lover and a fighter, Cassie Wyman thought I was cute, and I was coming to make my debut on stage right now!

Deep breath in, deep breath out.

Go!

And I stepped out into the bright lights.

The End

COMING SOON ...

scary
STUFF

Danger! Warning! Red alert! Another amazing, astounding, awesomely good Brian Hobble adventure is coming your way soon.

When we meet again, things are becoming really scary. I'm being haunted by ghosts and ghouls. In the middle of the night, I have to creep around a spooky graveyard infested with blood-sucking vampires, and hope that my parents won't find out. Even more scary, I have to pass a really hard maths test. If I fail, I'll lose all my friends, and even my girlfriend, and life as I know it will be over ...

THIS IS SCARY STUFF.

Are you brave enough to read it??!!!

thanks *n. thanx.* Gratitude, appreciation and acknowledgement of people who helped with this book.

Thank you to the May Gibbs Trust whose fellowship provided me with accommodation in lovely Adelaide, South Australia, while I started writing this book. Thank you again, Zoe Walton and the staff at Random House for your support of Brian Hobble and his stories. Once again thank you, Melissa Balfour – your editing was encouraging, demanding, detailed and invaluable, even when your messages began, 'I think this draft is great, *but . . .*'! Finally thank you to my family and friends who read drafts of *Awesome Stuff* and whose valuable feedback kept me going.
R.T.

Richard Tulloch *n.*
rich-ud tu-lick. An author
and a playwright.

Richard Tulloch is not an awesome genius;
he's just someone who likes making up stories. He
worked as an actor, theatre director, drama teacher,
playwright and screenwriter before taking up book
writing. He has won a number of Australian Writers'
Guild awards for his plays, which include *Year 9 Are
Animals* and stage adaptations of Robin Klein's *Hating
Alison Ashley* and Paul Jennings' stories in *Unbeatable!*
He has written for many TV series including *Bananas
in Pyjamas* and *New McDonald's Farm*.

He has also written over fifty children's books.
Awesome Stuff is the third in his series of novels about
Brian Hobble's bizarre adventures.

Like other writers, Richard Tulloch often tells lies to
make a story seem better, funnier or more exciting.
He has tried rock-climbing but is hopeless at it. He
has sometimes been interviewed on morning chat
shows on TV. His nose is quite big, but within the normal size range for an author of his age.

He has two grown-up children, lives with his wife in
Sydney and spends part of each year based in
Amsterdam. In between times he travels the world,
performing his storytelling show *Storyman* and teaching writing workshops in schools.